Julia Goddard

The Golden Journey

And other Verses

Julia Goddard

The Golden Journey
And other Verses

ISBN/EAN: 9783744798129

Printed in Europe, USA, Canada, Australia, Japan

Cover: Foto ©Andreas Hilbeck / pixelio.de

More available books at **www.hansebooks.com**

THE

GOLDEN JOURNEY

AND OTHER VERSES

BY

JULIA GODDARD

LONDON

LONGMANS, GREEN, AND CO.

1875

CONTENTS.

—◦◦◦—

	PAGE
THE GOLDEN JOURNEY	1
'MEMENTO DOMINE'	. 154
'JUSTUS FREIHERR VON LIEBIG IST GESTORBEN'	. 158
A REQUIEM	- 164

REPRINTED FROM 'ONCE A WEEK.'

A SONG IN JUNE	75
UNDER THE TREES	79
A PASTORAL .	81
FAIR MELISSA	87
THE SPOILER DESPOILED . .	95
HEIDELBERG	. 120
JUNE	133
JULY	137
OCTOBER	. 141
NOVEMBER	. 142
NEW YEAR'S DAY	145

vi
CONTENTS.

PAGE

The Burial of the Old Year . 14?

My Soul and I . . . 15(

REPRINTED FROM 'CASSELL'S MAGAZINE.'

To-morrow 7?

Daphne . . 8?

Wooing . ??

The Song . 9?

The Lost Flower 101

Spinning . 103

My Neighbour's Daughter 113

Love and Spring 13?

Yesterday . . . 151

The Felling of the Trees . 160

Bring Roses . 162

REPRINTED FROM THE 'ST. JAMES'S MAGAZINE.'

Not Lost . . . 105

A Legend of St. Cecilia . 108

The Two Sisters . . 116

On an Offer of Marriage . 126

N.B.—The Verses from the Magazines indicated are republished by the kind permission of Mr. William Bradbury, Messrs. Cassell, Petter & Galpin, and Messrs. Rivington.

THE GOLDEN JOURNEY

B

ANTWERP.

Chime of bells from the Cathedral.

.

MORNING.

MOURN for the dead!
Lift up your voice as she of old,
In Rama wailed, and wept aloud
For those she should no more behold.
  Mourn for the dead!

NOON.

  Mourn for the dead!
Mourn that the short life race is run,
The limbs in death laid stiff and cold,
Ere yet the longed-for goal was won.
  Mourn for the dead!

EVENING.

Mourn for the dead !
Mourn that the sands ran down ere eve
Had westward met the setting sun,
And earth was fair, too fair to leave.
Mourn for the dead !

MIDNIGHT.

Mourn for the dead !
Wake, sleeper, wake, lift up your song
Through night, whilst planets musical
Chime with the harp untouched so long.
Mourn for the dead !

Mourn for the dead !
Wake, sleeper, wake, lift up your cry,
That so the dead may live in song
For ever in men's memory.
Mourn for the dead !

So chimed the bells at Antwerp, morn, noon, and night
With their sweet silver tongue, all eloquent.
' Mourn for the dead ! uprear a monument

To him so sudden snatched from mortal sight,
Mourn for the dead, who sleeps in endless night.'
 So chimed the bells at Antwerp, from the tower,
All laced in stone, as though the sculptor's hand
Had fashioned it from some fantastic scroll,
Visioned to him in dream of fairy-land ;
Crocket and shaft and rose and angel-head,
All delicately carved into one whole
Of beauty, whose elaborate design
Grew threefold in each slender chiselled line.
 'Mourn for the dead !' the pealing bells still flung
Their words in music. 'Chant a requiem meet
For him who living, would have deathless sung
A melody so rare, that at his feet
The world had offered up its incense sweet.'
And he had won the longed-for wreath of bay
That poets wear ; he said, 'Twere nobler far
Than wearing royal crown, since kings but lay
Claim to an outer reverence ; though a king
'Mongst men were, sooth, no despicable thing.
Yet greater still the poet, he whose song
Leads all men onward, and makes dwelling-place
Within their hearts, and bows the trancèd throng,
With the full fervour of resistless grace.

Moves men to laugh, weep, grieve, rejoice with him,
With him to cast off hope, or rise sublime
To heights of faith that they had never reached
Had they not heard the poet's music chime.
So true that at his lightest word they thrill
With joy or pain according to his will,
And self-paid honour feel in honouring him.

And he had won that fame, for he had rare
Discrimination of all harmonies
Of sight or sound, that trembled in the air,
Or flushed the heavens, or breathed in sylvan sighs,
Floated in ambient clouds o'er summer skies ;
Or with the stars in mystic courses sang,
Or in weird notes throughout the forest rang ;
Or in the myriad lights and shades that fell
Upon the vine-clad hill and citadel,
When in the ruddy west the sun went down
In amber-streaked and crimson glowing sky
Behind the heights, above whose turret-crown
A flaming aureole shone so radiantly,
That tower and turret passed into a cloud
Of violet bursting from a golden shroud.

And he had sense of all the mysteries
That stir man's pulse, and link with subtle chain

The outer life to that which hath its rise
Within ourselves, and moves or heart or brain.
Its rise in us ?   Nay, from a higher source,
That binds us in indissoluble ties
With Nature, comes that undefinèd force,
That thus impels our inborn sympathies,
Outward to flow in yearning love to all
That He has made.   To turn towards all that brings
Us into contact with Himself again ;
Through the mute beauty of material things,
That still hold minor link in the great chain,
Wherewith humanity is held in thrall.
One whole creation circling 'neath His wings,
One God in us, above, around, in all.

     Alas ! alas ! I sang in days of old,
That life was beautiful ; that through it rolled
A river golden-waved and crowned with light,
Its depths with everliving waters fed,
That found in human hearts their fountain-head,
In hearts that looked upon the world aright.
A river bubbling up pure rills that stole
Over the parched up earth, and dewed the flowers,
As gracious words bedew the fainting soul
With magic moisture, until blooming bright,

In marvellous splendour, painted with the hues,
That mist dipped pencil from the rainbow caught,
Enchanted mortals ravished with the sight,
Fancied the buds from Paradise were brought,
And tended by the angels morn, noon, night,
To grace this world of ours with fair delight.

I sang that life was full of sweetest sound,
That ears attuned aright, no discord heard ;
But in the buzz of teeming life around,
One chord of hope and joy rang through the world.
I sang that life was glorious, that it grew
Into a psalm of beauty, whose clear note,
In unison mysterious with the quire
Angelic, higher heavenward doth float,
And its fair burden raised on seraph wings,
Lays at the footstool of the King of kings.

Yet even as I sang, a shadow fell
Across the life that I had painted fair,
And dimmed its glory with a blighting stain,
And blotted joy away and brought despair.
The sun dropped down behind the hills, and left
A heavy, leaden, starless firmament,
That darker grew.   And earth was all bereft
Of the life hum that filled it with content.

And lo! slow-moving wings the dull air stirred,
With heavy motion that oppressed my breath,
And chilled my heart ; and though no sound I heard,
I felt that through the gloom a Presence crept,
So dark, that all around, the shades of night,
Seemed to have paled away to sudden light.

   A solemn silence fell ; the air grew chill ;
My heart scarce beat, and fainter grew my breath,
And through the vague presentiment of ill,
I knew the awful Presence.   It was Death!

   I trembling bowed, although beside me stood
The fair Life-angel I had deemed divine,
The fair Life-angel I had worshippèd.
But altered now his character and mood!
Like some crushed bird down-beaten in his flight,
With drooping wings and bent, averted head,
And shuddering form, and eyes that once so bright
Had beamed, now lustreless.   Then sudden he
With bitter cry, his trembling wings outspread,
And fled away.
          And I was left alone
With Death, who, in discordant mocking tone,
Broke the dull silence.   'Mortal, bow the knee!
Life flees before me.   Wherefore strive with me?

What hope in life, since in the silent grave
Man finds an end of all the joys of earth.
The end of all his hopes, love, honours, mirth,
And all that erst a fitful radiance gave,—
Until my shadow fell across his path.
What joy in life? heart after heart yet breaks,
With wrench of parting; or with after-pain,
That comes in long, long days, and weary nights,
Wherein the loved and lost are mourned in vain.
That mingles with the daily task, and makes
The hand grow weary, and the heart grow faint,
Till joy's forsaken place sad patience takes.
" Not mine, not mine! take not my babe away!"
In piteous accent comes the mother's plaint.
Yet, Herod-like, I leave her desolate.
" Have mercy! mercy!" shrieks the 'wildered wife,
As the storm sweeps athwart the moaning sea;
E'en as she prays, sealed is her husband's fate, ,
For he has grappled limb to limb with me.

    ' Mortal! the world is mine.   The palace rears
'Gainst me no stronger walls, than crumbling shed;
The sunlight at my presence disappears,
And utter darkness o'er the land I spread,
The darkness of the heart, that mourns its dead.

O mortal ! then be Death thy theme to sing,
Death, stern, victorious, ruler over all :
Spreading o'er life a constant funeral pall,
The ever-conquering and unconquered king.'
    He paused ; but from my lips no answer came,
Though my sad heart in acquiescence bowed.
O Death ! men shudder at thy whispered name,
And how can I my trembling accents frame,
To sing of thee ?
                    Then all at once the cloud
That had enwrapped me faded, and mine eye
Fell on the work the painter gave to grace
The famed cathedral of his native place,
Limning the greatest death the world e'er knew.
And as I gazed, it seemed no picture there,
And o'er my soul a solemn wonder grew ;
The white folds fluttered round the powerless limbs,
From wounds afresh the blood began to flow ;
The thorny crown celestial radiance bore,
Causing a glorious light around to shine ;
Illuming that pale Face so touched with woe,
Whose visage marred as ne'er was man's before ;
Rigid in death, an awful beauty wore,
And death through Him had grown at once divine.

Death! death upon the cross so glorious!
And, lo, my wandering thoughts stole on apace,
To the disciples mourning o'er their Lord,
Not knowing whether all their faith had been
In vain.   What comfort could His death afford;
Had they not trusted in Him to redeem
His people Israel?   Now He had no place
Among the living.   Was it some dark dream
Or awful truth that they should see His face
No more.   Had they not watched His life ebb out,
Even as mortals', whilst the people's shout,
Rose: 'If thou be the Son of God, come down
And save Thyself!'   Till through the firmament,
Darkened to midnight darkness, pierced the cry,
' 'Tis finished!'—and the temple's veil was rent
Through that divine mysterious agony.
What hope had they?   Yet meekly still they wait,
Those sad disciples.   From the cross to bear
The body of their Master to the tomb.
For He was dead.   And they were desolate,
And earth and heaven for ever wrapped in gloom.

.   .   .   .   .

Still from the belfry tower the chimes pealed forth,
And through the great cathedral aisles their swell

Fell in sweet speech, as if fond hearts had breathed
Their hopes and fears into each silvery bell.
Or, as perchance immortal strain might float,
In diapason full with mortal blent ;
As though from earth uprose th' imperfect note,
Made perfect in the chord from heaven sent.

     'Mourn for the dead ! lift up your cry
     That so the dead may live in song
     For ever in men's memory.
      Mourn for the dead !'

Mourn for the dead ! The burden now for me
Had yet another utterance, that awoke
Through notes of sorrow a refrain of hope,
That ever into sweeter music broke.
How shall I sing a song ? The question came
E'en as it came to Hebrews tried, of old ;
When on the willow trees their harps they hung,
And wept as memory the past unrolled.
—What shall I sing ?
              Adown the nave I strayed ;
And, pausing near the western door, I read
The line that told the Antwerp blacksmith's tale.
But a brief line, and yet a theme it made
For the long tissue of romance I wove,

Of how the Antwerp blacksmith came to wed.
Of how brave Quentin Matsys won his love.
A pretty story sooth, and one that bare
A moral ; in these days a sequence rare.

　　Perchance e'en at this very western door
Had Quentin watched to see his love pass by ;
She as dew-spangled May-bud glittering fair,
With all the gauds of maiden bravery
In which can wealth fantastic fashion aid ;
Thick rustling silk of wondrous fine brocade
That lay in sculpture-like and massive fold ;
Gem-studded trinkets, chains of inwrought gold,
Soft ruby velvet, lace of Malines woof,
A lovesome picture for an artist-eye.
And how should Matsys' artist-soul be proof
'Gainst such a fair embodied phantasy ?

　　With air demure that might have graced a saint,
And down-dropped eyelids so she moved along,
Yet cast a searching glance among the throng,
Whilst quicker heaved the 'broidered boddice quaint,
As she, grown conscious of her lover nigh,
Met his fond gaze with answering look half shy ;
And deeper in her cheek the rose-flush burned,
And to her brow it mounted.   Then away

It died.   From earth to heaven she turned
Her thoughts, and kneeling down, she sought to pray.
    Say was it Satan tempting her aside
From holy thoughts to what towards earth did veer?
How could she 'twixt two loves her heart divide,
One tending heavenward, one that kept her here?
And so she fluttered, like a timorous bird,
That first his unproved wings would willing try;
Still clinging fondly to the parent nest,
Although he longs to cleave the upper sky.
Until she upward took her love with her,
And for two souls instead of one did plead.
It were no sin, she argued, at the throne
Of grace for those we love to intercede.
So prayed she that most perfect Love of all,
Over their love, their life, their death might fall,
And hold them ever in its golden thrall.
    But Quentin Matsys told not half his beads,
So was his mind distracted at the sight
Of her he loved; who filled his thoughts by day,
And flitted constant in his dreams at night.
For he who wrought in iron had a heart
Tender and true—a tongue full eloquent—

Was worshipful of her who prayed for him,
Adoring her with love all reverent.

Yet was his suit unprosperous.   When he spake
Unto her father, 'None,' the painter said,
Impassioned with his art.   'Nay, none but he
Who is a painter shall my daughter wed!'
Then Quentin Matsys turned away in grief
Since the beloved could never be his bride.
Never!   And then rose up his strength of will,
His love for her—the conscious artist-pride
In his own power.   Nay, why should not the skill
That had so dexterously in iron wrought,
Upon the canvas work with equal grace?
And kindled with the love-inspirèd thought,
He vowed, 'The blacksmith yet shall hold his place
Among the painters of his native town!'
And then, with anxious toil he patient strove
To mould his fingers through the force of love,
And to refine them to the subtler touch
That painter with his softer tools required.
To train his eye until the colours blent
In tints harmonious.   Till as if inspired,
He wrought; and 'neath his hand love guided grew
A wondrous picture, far his hopes above;

And then the painter said no more his ' Nay,'
And thus brave Quentin Matsys won his love !

    Out at the western door in open space
I passed, still pondering o'er the blacksmith's tale,
And straight before me stood the blacksmith's work ;
And many a lithesome girl had come, her pail
At Quentin Matsys' famous pump to fill.
Its canopy with twisted flowers entwined
In iron modelled with rare artist skill.
Aloft a warrior in full armour stood,
With glove in hand, as he a challenge threw
To those who scoff at what the hand may do
Moved by the heart. And in my musing mood
It seemed apt moral to complete the tale
That I had conjured up on ground-work frail.
    I wandered through the picturesque old town,
Whose streets bore many a trace of Spanish sway,
Where window-dotted roofs o'erhanging frown
O'er florid gables, till the smiling skies -
Seem but a slender line of smiling blue
That overhead in placid beauty lies.
    Still on and on until the river rolled
Before me, like a glistening sheet of gold

Kissed into glory by the setting sun.
And through the evening air the bells' soft swing,
Chimed with the rippling waters' murmuring;
Half sad, half sweet, the golden ripples sang,
Half sad, half sweet, the silvery bells still rang.
And chime and waters perfect music made,
Rising and falling in harmonious sweep,
A mournful melody that sprang from earth;
A strain of hope that had in heaven its birth,
And yet forbade not sorrowing man to weep.
And aye in solemn tones they spake,
'Mourn for the dead!   Lift up your cry,
That so the dead may live in song,
For ever in men's memory!
    Mourn for the dead!'

II.

TRÈVES.

THE old Red House at Trèves, with high-peaked roof,
And motto boasting Trèves' antiquity ;
And carven warriors armed all cap-à-pie,
Stern-gazing, as their weapons still were proof
To guard the splendour that in days gone by
Hovered around the ancient hostelry.
The ancient splendour that has passed away,
Yet left its shadow on the curious pile,
With gallery and court and gable graced ;
And nests of rooms and halls where grand array
Of senate pomp shone forth in former day.
Therein I sat and mused, and whilom traced
A picture, as is wont with them who dream ;
Till the far past did quite as near me seem
As that fair present yesterday effaced :

What matter if a cycle or an hour
Divides, when time has slipped beyond our power?
   Close to the market-place there stood a cross
Reared, so the legend runs, by Constantine,
In memory of the miracle that drew
His heathen soul to God, through fiery sign.
Upreared by Constantine!   The old world name
Had a strange charm.   Well better to believe,
In spite of sceptic, that he raised the stone.
Travellers are gainers if they can receive
The harmless myths that link us with the past,
Nor play too sternly the iconoclast.
Better believe too much than trust in naught,
Better admire too much than nothing praise;
Nay even wonder, since wise wonder's fraught
With childlike apprehension, that belongs
To wise men, not to fools; and he whose creed
Drives wonder far away hath greatest need
Of pity from his peers.   He who ne'er longs
To soar above what he can prove and state
Is so and so to strictest nicety;
Who would by rule and compass measure fate
And make a lifetime grasp eternity;
Measuring the Infinite by finite powers,

Forgetting man is but in babyhood,
. And but a nursery this world of ours
Wherein we strive for playthings in the dark.
For that our light is darkness scarce we mark,
Nor heed that man in ignorance doth wait
To pass to knowledge through Death's ebon gate.
    The old Red House at Trèves, at ancient Trèves,
The oldest town in all the German land,
What wonder that the burden of my stave
Should be the Past, since on the buried strand
That Time had billowed o'er, thought anchor cast
Deep down beneath the wave and wept the Past, the
       Past!
    And still I gazed upon the crowded street,
Noisy with busy tongues and pattering feet,
The sellers in the market-place,—the strife
Of haggling customers,—the measured tread
Of laden soldiers on their toilsome march,
Whilst martial music stirring influence shed ;
And with the thousand sounds and signs of life
That make a living world the air was rife.
Sudden mine eye fell on St. Gangolph's tower,
And round the clock the warning words I read

Of 'Vigilate et Orate!'—Watch
And pray, ere ye be numbered with the dead.
    Still dreaming—and the past from golden clouds
Unfolded, and sweet Fancy spread her wings,
And I was hurrying with the hurrying crowds
Towards the gorgeous palaces of kings.
'All hail, great Cæsar, hail!'   The echo died
And rose again, and floated through the air,
As the imperial train swept by in pride
Of pomp and power.   The glittering helm and spear
The costly bands of slaves, with perfumes rare,
And brows all garlanded with vine or rose.
And clashing music smote upon the ear ;
And mellow voices trolled a festal song,
'All hail, great Cæsar, hail!'   I gazed in awe
Upon the splendour of the iron sway
That Babylonia's king in vision saw
When silver, gold, and brass had passed away.
    Yet louder than the tide of mirth uprose
The roar of beasts, the agonizing cry
Of anguished nature in extremity.
My ears I stopped—my eyes I strove to close.
In vain.   The scene too vivid was portrayed.
Before me, but with crumbling walls no more,

The amphitheatre, as in days of yore,
Stood in its strength.   And crowded, rank on rank,
With eager gazers ; who the furious raid
Watched, that wild beasts on unarmed captives made,
And revelled in the death-throes of the Frank.
My pulse beat low, my heart within me sank,
'Pass barbarism hence!' and as I spoke
A softer picture on my vision broke.
A banquet hall, with noble guests arrayed
In gold and purple, who so late had gazed
Upon the scene of horror ; nor one throb
Had felt of pity as the eyeballs glazed
In death, and fainter grew the expiring sob,
Or at the shrieks, that rent the summer air,
Of frenzied victims wrestling in despair.
Now couched luxurious round the festive board,
Where amber wine from amber flasks is poured
By gliding slaves ; or from gold flagons dripped
In ruby drops into fair chalice set
With jewels worth the ransom of a king.
Or dainty meats the appetite to whet ;
And comfitures, rare fruit on salvers heaped—
Whilst singing waters from the fountain leaped,
And on a crystal sea their foam-drops flung

Or sparkled up in ever-bubbling pearls,
Mocking the song of flower-crowned singing girls;
And light flashed through the hall, and laughter rose
And tongues unloosed, as free the vintage flows.
Strange contrast all these sounds of festive mirth
To those that late rang o'er the startled earth !

    The vision fades, the palace disappears,
The amphitheatre in ruins lies,
And through the Porta Nigra's time-worn arch,
The swift, all undisturbed, on fleet wing flies,
Or builds her nest, where once the Roman guard
Over the ancient town kept watch and ward.
O Past! O Past! Man vainly makes his moan,
O'er thy insatiate grave unsatisfied.
If this and this had been—or I could live
Again my time, I should have wiser grown.
How many a trespass would I now forgive ;
How many a deed perform, I left undone ;
How many an idle word have left unsaid,
Or spoken that which had its guerdon won !
Oh dead and gone! and impotent we stand
Upon the fresh closed grave, and sorrowing weep.
Ah ! what avails the past ? for it hath fled,
And left us powerless with our buried dead,

With naught but bitter memory to fling
Its halo round us, as we vigil keep
Beneath the mournful shadow of its wing.

Within the fairest church of Trèves I stood,
And through the rich-stained windows in long rays
Of gold the sun came streaming, in a flood
Of light that tinted shadows set ablaze:
Then gently fell upon the pillared cross,
That on its slender shafts the Apostles bore,
A holy group.   Yet passing through, I moved
A-nigh the wall, and there I paused before
An image that my heart attracted more.
A dead Christ in the ghastliness of death—
The clay-cold limbs—the eyelids tightly pressed,
Tinged with the purple hue of livid death.
The while, the pallid lips, in rigid rest,
Told of the bygone sufferings of the Blest.
   It was no work of art, yet certain skill
Had made it natural, so that when I strayed
Away, almost unconsciously my will
Still brought me back and back again, and made
My spirit tremble with a gentle thrill,
That was half joy, and yet that half dismayed,

'Twas death I saw, death that I realised,
Shutting out hope from earth—yet into heaven
Opening the door of that perfectèd life,
Which through His death, Christ unto us hath given.

  Rouse up, ye slumberers, lest the moments prized
Too fleet shall flee. Arouse while yet 'tis day,
O 'Vigilate et orate!' Pray,
That ye may find the strait and narrow way
That leads up to the golden gates of heaven.

  The afternoon wore on. I musing turned
Into the great cathedral. Lower burned
The sun, and made the distant arches seem
Half shadow; and each taper's quivering beam,
Like unto restless star on hazy night.
And then I listened to the preacher's voice,
Amid a motley crowd of worshippers,
Who hung upon his words in rapt delight.

  'I am the Door; there is no other way
To enter into heaven. I am the door,
I was, am now, and shall be evermore,
The entrance to the fold. I am the Way,
I am the door. Come, weary ones, and I

Will let you in.'   Doth not the shepherd care
For his own flock?   When their parched tongues are
         dry,
He leads them unto waters gushing fair;
And when their limbs are weary, and their feet
Are torn and bleeding, then he lets them lie
Mid pleasant pastures, 'mongst the blossoms sweet;
And when the sun sinks down and night is nigh,
He gathers them within his fold to rest,
And they lie down in safety at his feet.

    'I am the Shepherd, ye are all my sheep,
And though ye slumber, yet I never sleep.
Will ye not hear my voice?   O come to Me,
For I will turn no sinful one away.
I stand and knock—the way to heaven is free;
I am the Light, the Life, the Truth, the Way.
Fear not.   None strays so far but I can find,
And bring him home.   None with a heart so sore,
But I in pity can his wounds up-bind;
None so deep sunk in sin, but I can pour
My peace upon him, if, with willing mind,
He comes.   O come, ye people, unto Me,
For I have paid your ransom with My life.
O come, ye worn and weary with the strife

Of earth.   Ye fearful ones and sore distressed,
Come unto me, and I will give you rest.
I am the door, there is none other way
To enter into heaven.   I stand and wait,
O listen to My voice ere 'tis too late !
—I am the Door.'

  The preacher's voice sank low,
As he pronounced the blessing ; and like wave
That restless heaves, throughout the crowded nave
The kneeling multitude swayed to and fro,
Yet all was silence.   Then with one accord,
Wailed out the voices in a solemn chord,
' Have mercy on us, Lord ! have mercy, Lord !'
  The fading sunlight fell in misty flood
Athwart the aisles, and lighted here and there
Some patch of gorgeous colour, contrast rare
With sombre grey ; and fragrant incense cloud
Curled into wreaths.   Beside the altar stood
The priest.   And pealing organ, sweet-voiced quire
Echoed from arch to arch.   And from the crowd,
In eager supplication humbly bowed,
Rose up in deep response, the wailing chord,
' Have mercy on us, Lord ! have mercy, Lord !'

And lo ! I worshipped with them, though I held
A different creed.   Yet creeds all died away,
Before the one great truth the preacher taught,
'I am the Door—I am the only Way.'
     I care not what their sect, if so they hold
That one great truth that unto man is given :
That, turning earth's theologies aside,
Will lead in safety to the courts of heaven ;
A bond of union—strong enough to bind
The differing world in bands of unity.—
A bond of union—strong enough to blind
Believing eyes to small diversity ;
The rallying cry from Heaven that guides alone
The Church Invisible throughout the world,
The parted army of the saints that makes
The only Catholic Church the Lord doth own,
O'er which the great white banner is unfurled.
     God only sees where that white banner waves,
Pure as the lily, fair as unstained snow,
Marked with a blood-red cross !   Yet, though unseen,
It floats above His people here below,
And underneath its folds they dwell in peace,
Off-shaded from the heat of fiery sun ;
And side by side march all unconsciously.

Nor shall they know till the great race is run,
How differences here shalt melt in one
Great harmony.   When in the light of day,
The day that knows no night, they then shall see
How that the Lord from many gardens plucked
The flowers that blossom in eternity.

  Ah ! what avail theologies men raise,
From some dogmatic section of the brain,
And points obscure endeavour to make plain,
Through reasoning intricate and subtle phrase !
The slender niceties that doctors teach
With all the technicalities of speech ;
The tedious formulas that men plan out,
With the preciseness of a pedant mind,
Nor yet this point with that can clearly bind ;
While Satan laughs at each hair-splitting doubt,
That leads men from the one great truth aside.
In labyrinthine folds their minds to vex,
He triumphs ; as unequal to decide,
They, betwixt light and dark their souls perplex
And so in chaos evermore abide.

  What matter to resolve if you or I
Elect, or through free-will the pathway try ?
What matter to involve one's self in doubt,

Of how sin in the world was brought about.
Enough that it exists—the object plain—
In that it is a curse, to root it out,
And a stout fight against it to maintain.
Why with such questions then the mind distress?
It is not meant that man should be all-wise,
Wait till the fruit of that fair tree we taste,
That bears anew, in fields of Paradise,
A fuller crop than when the serpent lay
Coiled up beneath its shade.   Till man restored
To the first Adam's blissful state shall stray,
In the new Eden planted by the Lord.

    We make religion but a science thus
By dogmatising.   But a body dead
To which the doctor's knife we careful bring
In order to dissect, ere we discuss
The point from whence vitality doth spring.
A matter of the brain, and not the soul,
Missing thereby the heaven-implanted fire,
Which is the godlike spark to move our whole,
To cause us ever heavenward to aspire.
Whose heat fanned to a flame shall glorious shine,
And shed around our path a light divine.
    Religion is that principle of faith

In God, that makes man act as though he saw
His Maker standing face to face with him,
And weighing every deed by His pure law
Of right.   E'en in the smallest thing
Making of God, his conscience and his king.
And he shall keep this faith unswervingly,
Who through the darkened watches of the night,
And midst the toil and trials of the day,
Can hear the voice of Him who cries alway,
'I am the Way, the Life, the Truth, the Light,
None cometh to the Father but through Me.'

    .   .   .   .   .   .

Thus musing, as the deepening night stole on,
I at the casement sat, whilst in the street
Died out the sound of busy tongues—and feet
Moved but at intervals.   The lights had gone
From out the neighbouring windows, one by one,
For sleep had waved his sceptre o'er the town.
And one by one the stars peeped out on high,
Like angel-eyes that watch the world asleep ;
And on St. Gangolph's tower the moon looked down
And traced in silver lines the warning cry
That man should ever in remembrance keep,
O 'Vigilate et orate.'—Pray

And watch, for time is speeding fast away,
To-morrow soon will be but yesterday ;
A yesterday some eyes shall sorely weep
That laugh to-day.   O Past ! aye growing old,
O weary Past that ne'er will cease to be ;
Though gathering Time within thy grasping fold,
Ne'er shortening by thy strides eternity !
O Past, O Past, the weary night is long,
When will the morning break and night have fled ?
And then a voice, like chime of far-off song,
I seemed to hear ; as answer from the dead.
' The Past shall never, never cease to be ;
What were the present if the past should flee ? '
And I was troubled half, half-comfortèd.
The voice went on, ' What were the future, say,
If by one touch the past were swept away ?
The past is builder of eternity.
Each trivial incident man counts as naught,
Is as a deftly fitting stone inwrought
Into the building of the life to be.
Each act of man's has life for evermore;
And what he puts in motion still goes on ;
His life-deeds move the world when he has gone,

D

Upbuilded by them to another shore.
Man knows not e'en the end of careless words,
That on and on and on, go muttering
Unto all time, a thousand meanings uttering
He thought not of; that into channels flee
He never reckoned on, nor where they flow,
Yet which in ceaseless course still onward go
Singing a song to all eternity!
Ah! were man's words of silver, and his speech
Of gold, how fair a melody might reach
Unto the haven; and like summer sea
Of music murmuring ripples, softly break
Athwart the harbour bar, and joyous wake
A sweet refrain from the angelic quire!
Ah! were man's deeds all of the lightsome day,
How fair a sun he in himself might shine!
Ah! were his heart pure as the spotless snow,
He might in heaven walk, ere the Divine
Had taken him from earth.'

                      'Can it be so
With any child of earth?' I eager cried.
But the voice answered not. And softly sighed
The bell from old St. Gangolph's tower, and brought

Its warning, as in answer to my thought,

O ' Vigilate et orate.'   Pray

And watch, for greater grows the Past alway,

—To-day with thee will soon be yesterday.

III.

THE MOSELLE.

THE morning rose with hazy light,
Nor yet had cast the veil away,
That winding round it through the night
  Fled with the perfect day.

Still is the river, calm and clear,
That flows along by ancient Trèves,
And darting swallows skimming near
  Their restless pinions lave.

The bridge that spans the fair Moselle
Is mirrored arch by arch below,
And boats with great white folded sails
  Bask in the morning glow.

Their colours gay, their painted prows
Are traced upon the glassy deep,
And boat and boatman seem to lie
    Lulled in a trancèd sleep.

Soft curtained by the morning haze,
That glamoured stillness round them flings,
And to the rose-stained light of dawn
    A tenderer shadow brings.

O river, fresh at morning's dawn
As childhood's dreaming early years,
When all is bursting into bloom,
    And laughed away are tears.

When e'en the darkest cloud scarce hides
Its inner edge of silvery hue,
But in a thousand rainbow dyes
    The sun comes peeping through.

Softly we sped adown the tide,
Between the golden fields of corn,
The reapers well their sickles plied,
    And fairer shone the morn.

Whilst mild-eyed oxen, yoked abreast,
With strong sleek limbs and measured pace,
In patient mood, their toil pursued
   With slow majestic grace.

We passed the Quint, whose chimneys tall
Tell of the brawny workers there ;
Past Mehring, with its red-peaked roofs ;
   Then grew the scene more fair.

The lovely hills rose up with wreaths
Of graceful quivering birch o'erhung,
And here a duskier line of beech
   A deeper shadow flung.

Whilst at their foot great walnut trees
Their giant branches stretched out wide,
And silver willows saw their leaves
   Clear-painted in the tide.

For though so fair the shimmering leaves,
So fair above the mountain dyes,
As fair a picture in the stream
   With them in beauty vies.

Are magic painters there below
To catch each ever-changing hue,
To fix it on the shining wave
   And charm the sight anew ?—

To catch each glint of purer gold
The sun sends down the mist to chase,
To bid each sleeping flower unclose,
   And earth unveil her face ?—

To catch each sign of gladsome life
And trace it on the sparkling flood.
Each bird, each fluttering butterfly,
   Each reed, each lily bud ?

The sun rides higher in the sky,
And from the river banks are heard
The hum of toil, the hum of song,
   The hum of life upstirred.

Past Ensch, past Ensch—the sun shines bright
And gently with the stream we glide ;
The peasants come, their pails to fill
   Down by the waterside.

The far hills melted into blue
Until they faded far away,
Whilst nearer tints of glowing green
   In varied beauty lay.

The vineyards stretched for many a mile,
From jutting rocks the vines sprang up,
Vine-country of the Brauneberg !
   Up ! fill the sparkling cup.

In honour of the fair Moselle,
The stream that nourishes the vine :
Vine-crowned be it for many a day,
   And pledged in golden wine.

Fill high the cup ! wreathe roses round :
For man at noon is in his prime,
And life is sweet, and hopes are bright,
   He takes no thought of time !

So glided we past famed Pisport,
Past Kasten's church and Mühlheim town,
And paused, where high o'er Berncastel
   Its ruined Burg looks down.

Hark ! shots are fired—hark ! music's strain,
Garlands and banners flutter gay,
The guns flash out ; and merry shouts
    Proclaim a festive day !

The Schützenfest.   Ay, laugh and sing
Make life as joyous as ye may—
Wherefore of sad to-morrows reck,
    Whilst happy is to-day ?

Ah ! so it is for aye and aye,
Men laugh to-day, to-morrow die—
And still the world goes on while they
    Dead and forgotten lie.

Ah ! so it is for aye and aye;
Half the world laughs, half sadly weeps,
Whilst onward to eternity
    The river silent sweeps.

Now fairy glints of wooded heights,
And quaint grey towers whose sombre dye
The golden green acacias grace,
    We idly floated by.

Where bright catalpas, in their prime,
Clusters of rosy blossom spread ;
And still beneath the purple hills,
    Our dreamy course we sped.

Beneath the hills whose leafy shade
Is tinged with ever-changing mist
Of sun-touched glory, like a pall
    Of gold or amethyst.

Ah ! is not life a ceaseless song,
A careless floating down the stream ?
For youth is brave, and manhood strong,
    Life is a happy dream.

Past Wolf—the ruined convent lies
Above us—hence sad thoughts away !
When nature breathes sweet life around,
    Why muse upon decay ?

Hill enfolds hill in soft embrace
Till parted by the silver tide ;
Then start to sight the slender spires,
    Or grey-roofed Dorf they hide.

Trarbach ! The Gräfinburg up-built,
By Starkenburg's brave-hearted dame
With ransom from Trèves' prelate proud,
  All honour to her name!

Past Briedel nestled 'neath the hills ;
Past picturesque black-timbered Zell ;
Then on to Alf, whose stream runs swift
  To join the blue Moselle.

The blue Moselle, the winding stream
That glides 'twixt verdant banks along,
Past convent, hamlet, deep ravine,
  And wooded slopes among.

Now lovelier still, thou deep ravines,
A glimpse of fairy-land reveal ;
And sunbeams slide in amber streaks,
  And singing streamlets steal

All in and out, with silver flash,
Among the ferns. On darting wings
The dragon-fly an emerald trail
  Above the water flings.

Yet on and on, we cannot stay ;
Past Beilstein's ruined towers we glide,
And deftly curves, and deftly winds
　　The silent-flowing tide.

And steering round a wooded point,
With hills still rising, height on height,
The fairest scene bursts on our view
　　As Cochem comes in sight.

One castle rising o'er the wave
As though to guard the ancient town—
One castle on the mountain height
　　Uprears its turret crown.

Around, the everlasting hills
With warm sun-painted colours glow,
And vine-hung rocks their beauty cast
　　Into the stream below.

O picture that in Memory's clasp
Shall nigh my heart for ever be,
Sweet vision echoing a past
　　That ne'er returns to me !

Still on adown the dreamy tide—
And o'er old Alken's linking wall,
On Thurant's tower the deepening shades
    Of evening softly fall.

On, past bold rocks whose jutting brows
Conjure up many a goblin tale,
And lower sinks the setting sun
    All in a golden veil.

Past Gondorf's château, till we reach
The castled heights of fair Cobern,
And ever lower in the sky
    The crimson sun did burn.

And as it touched the purple peaks,
One dazzling sheet of light unrolled
And tinged the Cross upon the height
    With its last tint of gold.

O token fair ! as though the sun,
Though dying, still its light would fling
O'er the most precious sign on earth
    To which man's soul doth cling.

O river, river! dark at eve,
Dim shadows vaguely o'er thee creep,
As shadows that in life forewarn
  Of man's last sweetest sleep.

O river, river! dim and dark,
Whose depths no mortal eye can see ;
So life rolls on, nor can we mark
  Its hidden mystery.

Rises the solemn silver moon
On towns embowered in orchards, shines
And falls upon the silent waves
  In silver rippled lines.

Shines on the town of famed Coblenz
That rears its towers above the Rhine—
Crown of the vine-land, where at last
  Moselle and Rhine entwine.

Like twin-souls, wandering through the world
To find their mates, the rivers sighed,
Long time apart—until their floods
  Met, never to divide.

Twice seven are the arches tall,
That graceful span the fair Moselle,
And ivory white each buttress gleamed,
   As white the moonbeams fell.

Beneath twice seven arches tall,
By Coblenz town the waters glide,
And twice seven ebon archways cast
   Black shadows on the tide.

O river! lost at eventide
In depths of dreamy silver mist,
Fair as that golden haze at morn
   Through which the sunlight kissed

The earth until at length it woke
With rosy blush to life and light,
Called out of darkness—now again,
   Fast fading into night.

So mystery at either end,
Of life's strange current, shrouds our days--
Death's midnight shadows cloud the stream
   That rose in morning's haze.

O river fair! thy course is run,
And vanished as a summer dream,
The gilding sun, the flowers that decked,
   The weeds that clogged, thy stream.

So dream-like shall earth-glories fade,
So as a dream earth-griefs be o'er,
When the life-river's waves shall break
   Upon th' eternal shore!

O river, river! flowing from the South,
Came ye far south enough to tell
How the blue waters of the Tyrrhene Sea
Ring out a solemn and unceasing knell
For him who in his lonely grave is sleeping?

O river, river! flowing from the South,
Came ye far south enough to hear
The sultry south-wind breathe a constant sigh
For him who far from all he held most dear
Lay down and died and left the loved ones weeping

O river, river! flowing from the South,
Came ye far south enough to see
A mountain burning with its fitful fire,
Beneath the sunny skies of Italy,
Lighting the grave of him who there lies sleeping?

O river, river! flowing from the South,
Came ye far south enough to know
That a bright angel spreads his peaceful wings
Above the grave, and comforts those below,
Whisp'ring, 'The sleeper rests in Heaven's keeping!'

IV.

THE HARZ.

GHOSTS, goblins, spectres, phantoms, what are they
But offspring of the rude barbaric mind?
The first assertion of the spirit sway
That rules man's being ; and the undefined
Acknowledgment of that strange inner self,
That other fuel needs to feed the fire
Than mere materialism ; and itself to link
With supernatural essence doth aspire.
    Smile not in lofty wisdom, O ye wise
Philosophers ! at that poor untaught wight
Who trembles as the shadowy dusk draws near,
Nor dares to pass the lone graveyard at night,
Lest the pale ghost of some lost friend who lies
Entombed may sudden to his sight appear,
Or lest his name, called by some spirit passed

Into another world he there might hear.
Smile not, ye wiser ones!—it is the first
Instinctive inkling of a future life ;
A recognition that the spirit lives,
Though passed beyond this scene of mortal strife ;
Can still preserve identity, nor yet
Those that it communed with in life forget ;
And, though in spheres beyond our mortal ken,
It yet is linked in sympathy with men.

    Ay, all the old-world superstition proves
That man with spirits fain himself would bind,
As feeling that within his breast there moves
Something that he in unison doth find
With spirit-life. And so he sets his brain
To work at midnight ; in the lone weird hour,
Wherein 'tis held the spirit-world hath power,
And peoples nature with a motley train
Of ghosts and goblins. Or it so may hap
That he, full-gifted with poetic vein,
May rest his head in gentle Fancy's lap,
And, soothed to sleep by her magician-hand,
Fall straight a-dreaming of the Elfin-land.
How through the forest, at Midsummer-tide,
When scarce the sun leaves darkness on the earth

Sufficient for the tender moon to hide
With her soft beams—how Oberon would ride
In gay procession with his courtiers forth,
To meet his longed-for wilful fairy bride;
And in the midst of revelry and mirth,
And beauty bursting out on every side,
With Elfin splendour touch the moonlit earth,
Till herb and flower with magic lustre glow,
And fuller loveliness at midnight show
Than e'er in blazing noontide light was seen;
All to do honour to the fairy queen.
For her the foxglove rang its crimson bells
With silver tongue forged at the fairy forge;
For her the crystal streamlets jocund poured
Mellifluous music through the mountain gorge;
For her the Lady Slipper shrank its bloom
Of spotted velvet to dimensions meet
To suit the symmetry of fairy feet.
And butterflies, with gold and purple wings,
Or dashed with scarlet, silken saddles bore,
Whereon her saucy pages loved to ride,
And aye, more jauntily their plumed caps wore,
And now and then a dainty oath they swore,
Yet under breath—for sharp the penalty:

Since culprit sprites were sentenced for a space
In flowering Fly-catchers to take their place,
Whose cruel thorns their tender bodies tore.
Or, if a gentler judgment were assigned,
They, in the mouths of huge Snap-dragons caught,
Were held up to derision, while they sought
In vain their blushes and chagrin to hide.
    Whilst fays more virtuous, on azure wings,
Athwart the tinted moonbeams glide and slide,
Till tossed by careless slip on softest bed
Of feathery moss, with sparkling light supplied,
That round the brilliant fireflies fitful shed.
Others held festival in Lily isles
That floated on the clear translucent stream ;
Others in glittering train, on fairy steeds,
Flashed through the forest, like a sunlight gleam,
To hunt the mortal forth who dare come nigh
And into Elf-land's secrets seek to pry :
But finding him a Poet, changed their ire
Into sweet sympathy, and loving crept
A-nigh, and whispered in his ears weird tales,
Their loves, their joys, their sorrows, as he slept,
Until his heart to rapture strung, he wept
At the wild beauty so intense and deep

That blossomed round him in his charmèd sleep.
And still he slept beside the murmuring stream,
And learned of Elf-land in his golden dream ;
And through deep draughts of wonder and delight
Upsprang a poet's fair Walpurgis Night.

    Then waking, scattered he the myths around
That thus into his soul had entrance found ;
And all men listened to the cadence sweet
That rolled in song-tide from the poet's lips ;
And in their heart it had a luscious taste,
As honey that the bee from fragrance sips—
It bore them mere humanity beyond,
Raised a creation fairer than their own,
And o'er their ruder and uncultured souls
The poet had a gracious influence thrown,—
A sense of spirit-life in beauty sown.

    Fair are the mountain forests of the Harz,
Whose pine-trees rear their giant stems as masts
All hung with sails of fringèd foliage ;
Or like the columns in cathedral vast,
Their capitals with plumaged green bedecked,
Their slender branches arched in graceful line,
E'er pointing upward, as though Nature's hand

Close copying Art's more regular design
Were lovesome to the Gothic architect.
Through the sparse rifts the blue sky peeping came,
And shreds of gold lay tangled here and there
Upon the moss, like splinters of sun-flame ;
Or blazed upon the rocks, in colours rare.
The wild bees hummed, the waters stole along,
And Nature murmured in harmonious song.
Whilst from afar rang clear the cattle-bell
In short staccato notes, a lively strain
Jerked out capriciously, with sweet disdain
Of time i' the cadence ; yet it soothing fell
Upon the ear as nigher still it drew
And mingled with the horn the herdsman blew
To call the cattle home.   In steady line
With tinkling bells the large-eyed sober kine
Gravely towards the village wend their way ;
And one by one, as home by home is neared,
Lessens the flock ; the music fainter grows,
And herd and herdsman weary seek repose.

The Harz, the fatherland of spirits wild,
Lay fair before me, a weird tract outspread
Of forest-covered mountain, granite rock,

And torrents dashing from their mountain-bed.
A wondrous fairyland that held my soul
In rapture, whilst a thousand legends stole
Upon the winds around, or whispered through
The flutt'ring birchen trees ; or found a tongue
In quiv'ring willow, or with louder note
By chattering brook or waterfall were sung ;
Till blent in chorus rose their voice to tell,
How a fair Princess, once upon a-time,
Rode a wild race among these scenes sublime,
Over the huge rocks fled in wild despair,
Chased by her giant suitor, who would win
A bride, e'en though her love were given elsewhere.

  On the pursuer came—she, full of fear,
Yet strung to madness, still her course held on.
Height after height her gallant steed hath cleared,
Until in desperation she has won
The rock that overhangs the valley fair,
The Bode-valley.   Beauty everywhere—
Hill interlocking hill, and far away
Dying in tender blue.   And forests vast
Stretching out southward, yet she saw them not,
Her eyes were on the depths beneath her cast,
Where 'neath the crag a foaming torrent roared.

She paused. Hark! hark! like thunder crashing near
Sounded a horse's hoofs. Swift as the wind,
Her soul absorbed by one great blinding fear
That overcame all other sense, behind
She glanced ; and straight a giant form espies,
That ever greater grows against the skies.
Is there no hope ? One cry of utter woe,
One shuddering look at the abyss below,
One shuddering look across the chasm wide,
Then urging quick her steed to the mad spring,
One moment in the air, the next all safe
Upon the opposite rock his hoofs sharp ring.
Baffled, the Giant pauses—filled with rage.
It were unmanly thus to lose his bride ;
And furiously he spurs his courser on
To take the leap across the valley wide.
One frantic effort,—but the goal to miss—
Horseman and horse are plunged in the abyss.
    So runs the story—true or false, why care?
Or if the Bode river took its name
From bearing on its waves grim Bodo's corse,
Let the *Ross-trappe* keep its ancient fame,
Whilst the rude hoof-prints of the Princess' horse
Still mark the rock in witness of the tale.

O Harz! fantastic legends conjuring up!
Wild visions based on supernatural lore
Wherein the marvellous holds regal sway,
And which some would-be-wise ones grave deplore,
And sit and sigh and call their fellows fools,
Who care to list to such unlikely tales.
And yet perhaps some lessons we may learn
From fables, where a deeper learning fails.
O Harz! fantastic fancies conjuring up!
Ghosts, goblins, witches, in unearthly guise,
The powers of hell, the prince of darkness, flit
In medley strange before the myth-bound eyes;
Giving a shape to evil through that law,
That binds on man below to know and feel
The power of Evil tempting in the world;
And from that power, which thus itself reveals,
To start in horror.
                    Ay, such thoughts will rise
As on the *Hexentanzplatz* fair I stand,
And overlook the spirit-haunted land.
The Witches' Ball-room! sooth a lovely spot
To choose for revels.   Even that they might
The loftier Brocken ever keep in sight
That rises in the distance, o'er the peaks

Of green and purple hills that, fold on fold,
Are waked to flame in that great burning gold
That lights the sun as he his chamber seeks.
Below, the Bode through the valley wound
In bubbling crystals, whilst behind me lay
The terraced forests Treseburg that crowned.
The Witches' Ball-room!   Ah, at close of day
Grown fairer still, ceiled with the night-blue sky,
And all the hills and vales soft bathed in light
Flung from the pale moon's silver lamp on high :
And here the witches revel, save when they
To the great Blocksberg on Walpurgis-night,
A reckless rabble, take their boisterous flight
To meet their master ; and to dance away
The snow that lies there on the first of May.
The peasant knows that ne'er at Walpurg-tide
Is seen that bird of mischief, black and white,
Since magpies are the steeds that witches ride
Unto the Brocken on Walpurgis-night.
And so he nods and winks, his head wise shakes,
Yet scarcely dares to give his knowledge vent,
Lest for loose tongue he meet with punishment.
But rye from out three blooming fields he takes,
And with it goes to church, that so his eyes,

Oped by the triple charm, may there discern
The witches seated round, with butter-churn
Or pail upon their heads ; for in such guise
To the initiated they appear
For Sundays two after their impious feast
Upon the Brocken.   Yet he must depart
Quickly from church ere yet the solemn priest
The parting blessing doth pronounce, if he
Would from their vengeful wrath in safety be.

  Whence spring such myths save from the mystic
      mind,
After the supernatural inclined,
That fain into th' invisible world would search,
And twist all nature to some spirit end;
Instinctive feeling that material things
Must to the spiritual ever bend ;
Instinctive feeling that around us move
The powers of evil ; as if through the world
There ran the legend of lost angels hurled
To depths of misery from heights of love.
Throughout all nations, all mythologies,
Some such tradition runs.   The Vedas tell
How, led by Mahasoor, the Dewtahs rose,
And failing in their wild rebellion fell,

For ever by a threefold god pursued.
Of Ahriman, the Persian sage narrates,
How he to equal Mithras did aspire
(Mithras, the star of day, the friend of man),
Bringing upon himself celestial ire,
And from the regions of eternal light,
Was driv'n to chaos and to endless night.

Thus many a legend old we curious trace,
That hath a slender touch of truth for base,
But mounts in superstructure fanciful,
All overdone with gewgaws and odd freaks
Of whim-full builder, who has lost his plan;
And to repair the loss thus vainly seeks
By adding and augmenting as he can,
Yet, wandering ever farther from the source
Grows unintelligible, more complex.
So man by nature gropes his way along,
Still finding subtle mysteries to perplex,
Which he, though ever searching, ne'er finds out.
And so the spirit struggles on in throes
Of weariness, until the day is spent
In one long wail of impotent lament,
And round man's soul the deep night shadows close.

He vainly gropes without the gates of light,
Like the wild wandering Will-o'-wisps we see,
Declared with simple pathos by the myth
The souls of unbaptisèd babes to be,
That wander through the forests, deserts drear,
And lead the traveller on where water lies,
Hoping that he will pity on them take,
And Christian-like their Christless souls baptise,
That they no more may weep outside the gate,
But joyful enter into Paradise.

So through a Higher Help must men essay
To reach the light through the dark shades of eve
That gather round us in this border-land,
From which we wistful strive to gain a glimpse
Of that immortal life none can conceive ;
Yet that the soul with loving longing paints
So exquisite in beauty, that it fain
Would burst the gate that shuts the flood of light
From mortal-clouded and imperfect sight,
And the full vision of its glory gain.

V.

THE BROCKEN.

THROUGH lonely forests where the Ilse pours
Its waters in continual waterfall,
Leaping adown with waves of foaming white,
With roar melodious and musical ;
As if from slumber waked, each water-sprite
Were shouting in excess of wild delight
At the down-bursting of the silver flood
That shivered over green mossed rocks, or slipped
O'er shining stones, to choice enamel chased
Of rainbow colours, as the water dripped
Upon them.   Overhead the swaying pines
Waved their great boughs, rich with pink tasselled
        cones,
And frosted o'er with lichen white, that mocked
The handiwork that hoary winter owns.

Whilst nestling at their roots the oak-fern crept,
The purple-fruited bilberry beneath,
And orchis buds with nodding harebell vied,
And wood geraniums twined a starry wreath
Of crimson 'mongst the grass, that half did hide
The trumpet moss, whose horns the elfin band
Blow mellow tunes upon in Fairyland.

    Past towering Ilsenstein, upon whose crest
Is reared a cross, perchance to scare away
The imps that round its summit loved to play,
And fright the sleepy night-owl in its nest.
Wilder the torrent leaps through beechen shades,
Or birchwood, or 'neath ever-living pines
As steep and ever steeper grows the way—
And all is fair, so fair that one inclines,
Moved with the sight of loveliness around,
To half believe that earth hath reached the bound
Of God's creative beauty—and the heart,
Filled with deep joy through earth, begins to fear
The joys of heaven—and all that chains it here
To claim a greater and more loving part.

    'Ah! I shall miss the blooming trees of earth
That in the breeze their boughs luxuriant wave,

And I shall miss the memory-haunted flowers
That blossom o'er my grave.

And I shall miss the sound of waterfall,
The trickling of the many-voicèd rills ;
The glorious lights and shadows falling fair
Upon the distant hills.

And I shall miss the radiant hues that flush
The morning skies, or fade at eventide ;
And I shall miss the shadowy hours of night
That day from day divide.

No night ! no starry night ! No sun, no moon,
Yet light ! How can I picture light more fair,
How in my eyes half closed in finite sight
Can heaven with earth compare ?'

Peace, wailing heart ! Oh hush ! each unwise thought,
Can He not fashion fairer worlds than this ?
Cannot the Hand that out of chaos wrought
Such beauty, calling forth ecstatic bliss
In thy imperfect state ; when thou shalt be
Perfected, shall He not prepare for thee

A home so glorious that thy wondering eyes
Shall see re-won the long-lost Paradise ?

Wilder the mountain scene.   In blackened rings
The charcoal burners left their dusky trace,
Or 'neath roofed piles of wood slow burned the fires
And Kobold-like peeped out the grimy face
Of peasant toiling at the sylvan trade.
And steeper grew the path ; and bolder still
The rocks stood out, like giants turned to stone ;
Dwarfed was the pine-growth, and the air grew chill
And lo, it seemed as we had left below
Sweet Summer in the valleys, and had met
Old Winter waiting on the mountain height,
Watching for leaves to drop, and sun to set
The earlier, so that he might wing his flight
To deck his earth bride with a veil of white.
Higher !   The stately forests lay below,
And far beyond the billowy land out-rolled,
Like a dull sea all dusky-waved and cold,
Beneath a canopy of leaden grey
Untinged by sunset hues.   Obscured the sun.
Save when one flashing flame of crimson fire
Had shaped itself to semblance of a cross

That superstitious ones might take for sign ;
For portent of some miracle to come,
Foreshadowed by the hand of the Divine.
   Then died away the light ; the colour died
From the wild sweeps of heather at my feet,
'Mongst which the magic Hexenbesen raised
Its feathery tufts.   The last faint shadows fleet,
And earth and heaven in growing darkness meet.
Night, starless night came on, and wrapped in gloom
The Brocken, and the world that lay below,
And all was chill and silent as the tomb,
And in my heart prophetic sounded, ' Woe,
Despair, and death, for ever mortals' doom.'

   .   .   .   .   .   .

Morn rose upon the Brocken chill and grey,
And scarce the waning moon through misty veil
Traced out the edges of her crescent pale—
Beneath me rolled their billows wave on wave,
Hiding the mountain peaks ; a cloud-built sea
That far away illimitable stretched
Like shoreless ocean of eternity—
A silent sea—no sound of angry roar
Of waves, no gentle murmuring of the tide,
No sea-gull white to wing his flight to shore,

No white sail on its heaving breast to glide
And give one touch of life death's shadow dark to
      hide.
   Morn! but no sungates on their hinges roll
To loose Earth from the death-like bands of night
And whisper Easter-peace unto my soul.
Morn! but no sun, no light, no glorious light,
All dark!
          Then sudden, mist veils struggling through,
A dull red phantom glare was visible,
Nearer it moved full swiftly, and at last
Into an orb of crimson glory grew
That battled with the floating clouds, and cast
Its rays around, the mist wreaths to dispel;
And ever higher in the heavens it sped,
Threw crimson stains upon the dull grey sea,
And one by one each mountain reared its head
Like emerald island in an opal lake;
And one by one each valley struggled free,
From hiding clouds. And Shierke, Elend break,
With their huge spectral rocks all dimly out,
Recalling Faust and Mephistopheles,
Up-journeying to join the witches' rout.
   Far to the left the hills rolled towards the south,

Far to the north stretched out a great wide plain,
Town-dotted, where the Ilse twined along
A thread of silver, in and out again
In many a freakish twist.   And sunlight fell,
Bright sunshine on the earth with rosy ray.
Morning, fair morning! For the orb of day
Had drawn the trembling mists unto himself,
And loving chased each wandering cloud away
To its lost place in heaven, where now it lay
Bathed in the ruddy gold that gleamed above,
And flooded golden all the earth below
In resurrection garb.   Earth sprang to light,
Embraced in arms of everlasting love,
And blushing in the heaven-born morning glow
Forgot for ever the dark tomb of night.

I stood upon the Brocken tower alone
And viewed the scene so fair around me spread,
The blinding mists and clouds that veiled the earth,
In heaven's o'erpowering light all vanishèd.
    I stood alone and silently did pray,
'O Lord, so let it be in that Great Day,
When Thou shalt unto man Thyself reveal,
And take away the clouds that o'er our souls

Hang, and thy love and justice half conceal.

Then, what is now so dark make clear to us;

Open our eyes to see Thee face to face,

Not through a glass, but with a strengthened sight

In which we may at length Thy goodness trace,

And prove all mercy that so hard seems now.

Oh may Thy gift of sight to us light up

With unobstructed ray each wept out woe,

And turn the dregs of memory's bitter cup

To draught most sweet, that through Thy love did flow

Though we unheeding in our blind estate

Had not the power to comprehend that love;

But in our darkness mourning cruel fate

Cast down our eyes, nor saw the light above.

O Lord! O Lord! when that Great Day shall come,

And through the trembling earth the trumpet blast

Of the archangel sounding forth shall call

The quick and dead to meet the Judge at last;

When all the loved and lost we long have wept

Shall stand in living flesh before the Throne—

Lord! may we find our loved ones safe with Thee;

And for thy children, Lord, us also own.'

Alone I stood. Yet not alone, for God

Himself was with me in that lonely hour.
Alone ! yet not alone, for all around
Were angel-messengers full-armed with power,
And watchers from the world invisible.
Alone, yet not alone ; my soul was bound
In close communion with that other world,
And o'er me fell a sense of peace profound.
The golden gates were opening to my sight,
Far far aloft rich set with pearls they swung,
And a sweet sudden strain of music swept
Through space, soft dropping from the silver tongue
Of angels that in Paradise rejoiced
O'er one who late on earth had fall'n asleep
To wake in heaven.   And though I listening wept,
My soul with seraph quire a joyful measure kept.

SONG OF THE ANGELS.

Why weep ye for the dead as those which have no hope?
The Lord hath risen !
The Lord hath opened wide the gates of heaven,
And the strong bands of death asunder riven—
    Mourn not the dead !

Why weep ye for the dead ?   They know no weeping,
But loving wait

For those on earth left desolate and sorrowing
To join them in their glorious estate—
　　Mourn not the dead !

Why weep ye for the dead ?　The Lord hath taken
Into His care
Your treasures, where nor rust nor moth can enter,
And ye shall, waking, find them garnered there—
　　Mourn not the dead !

Why weep ye for the dead ?　Ye are but parted
For a short space.
When Death shall kiss your closing eyes to glory,
Then shall ye see the loved ones face to face—
　　Mourn not the dead !

Blest are the dead !　The King hath called them to Him,
Their troubles cease,
And He hath called them unto living fountains,
And all is life and light and perfect peace—
　　Mourn not the dead !

MISCELLANEOUS POEMS

A SONG IN JUNE.

THE brook went rippling, rippling,
　Over the pebbles in June,
Through reeds and rushes it wound its way,
　Humming a low sweet tune.
The little forget-me-not listened,
　And her blue eye beamed less bright,
And the startled lily oped wider
　Her flowers of gleaming white.
　　'O brook ! O brook ! now tell me
　　　What thou to the flowers didst say ?'
　　But the brook still rippling, rippling,
　　　Went lazily on its way.

The wind went sighing, sighing,
　Through the tall trees in June,
And the chestnut blossoms shivered
　As it sang its mournful tune.

The dove cooed ever more gently
  As the whispering wind passed by,
And the linnet's note sounded softer,
  And sadder the bittern's cry.
        ' O wind ! O wind ! now tell me
          What thou to the birds didst say ? '
        But the wind still sighing, sighing,
          Through the forest stole away.

My heart was beating, beating,
  Faster that day in June,
And a voice within it murmured
  A dreamy dirge-like tune.
' O heart ! O heart ! now tell me
  What the voice to thee doth say ? '
And my heart did sadly answer,
  ' All things must pass away.'
        And the brook went rippling, rippling,
          The wind sighed over the lea ;
        But the voice in my heart sounded sweeter
          The longer it sang to me.

TO-MORROW.

THE setting sun, with dying beam,
 Had waked the purple hills to fire ;
 And citadel, and dome, and spire,
Were gilded by the far off gleam ;
 And in and out dark pine-trees crept
Full many a slender line of gold ;
 Gold motes athwart the river swept,
And kissed it as it onward rolled.
 And sunlight lingered loth to go.
Ah well ! it causeth sorrow
 To part from those we love below,
And yet the sun as bright shall glow
  To-morrow.

The tide was ebbing on the strand,
 And stooping low its silver crest,
 The crimson seaweed laid at rest
Upon the amber-ribbèd sand,

Dashed o'er the rocks, and on the shore
Flung parting wreaths of pearly spray,
　Then fled away.   Yet turned once more
And sent a sigh across the bay,
　As though it could not bear to go.
Ah well ! it causeth sorrow
　To part from those we love below,
Yet thitherward the tide shall flow
　　To-morrow.

Two hearts had met to say farewell
　At even when the sun went down ;
　Each life-sound from the busy town
Smote sadly as a passing-bell.
　One whispered, ' Parting is sweet pain,
At morn and eve returns the tide.'
　' Nay, parting rends the heart in twain.'
And still they lingered side by side,
　And still they lingered loth to go.
Ah well! it causeth sorrow
　To part from those we love below,
For—shall we ever meet or no
　　To-morrow ?

UNDER THE TREES.

UNDER the trees in summer time,
    Under the chestnut trees,
  Looking up into their cool green shade
  By a thousand layers of green leaves made,
When the clustering flowers are past their prime,
    And the idle wandering breeze
  Slyly shakes the branches to and fro,
  And brings down a shower of summer snow
In the golden summer time.

Under the trees in summer time,
    Under the trees I lie,
  Peeping up into their boughs to see
  If the sun can dart down one ray on me ;
Whilst drowzily sounds the sheep-bell's chime,
    And the babbling brook goes by ;

And the birds sing cheerily many a tale,
Whispered to them by the passing gale
In the golden summer time.

Under the trees in summer time
      I lie and dream of thee,
   And I dream that in days to come, thou and I
   Shall meet again as in days gone by,
When laughing summer is in her prime,
      Beneath the chestnut tree ;
   When the listening breezes may tell each bird
   The sweetest secret that ever it heard
In the golden summer time.

A PASTORAL.

I

WHERE soft grey hills in summer sheen
    All purple-stained and streaked with gold,
All vermeil dashed, and tender green,
    Their image in the lake behold.

II

Where 'midst fair pastures browse the sheep,
    Where bird and butterfly disport,
Where 'mongst the brambles roses creep,
    And life seems but a summer thought.

III

Where by its dam the lambkin plays,
    Or crops the herb, or light frisks by,
Reminding of those olden days
    When shepherds reigned in Arcady.

G

IV

Where far away the eagle soars,
    Scared by the shepherd from the flocks,
Where babbling streamlet idly pours
    Over the moss-enamelled rocks.

V

O Phyllis, come ! the wild thyme sweet
    Shall offer incense at thy shrine ;
The warbling birds thy presence greet,
    And deeper homage yet be mine.

VI

The skies are bright, and blossoms rare
    Flora in loving frolic flings,
Since Zephyr stirs the balmy air
    With the soft waving of his wings :

VII

And far and near their silvery mirth
    Wakes up the hills and vales from sleep,
And o'er the beauty-laden earth
    A fresher sense of joy doth creep.

VIII

O Phyllis, come ! Earth's rapturous voice
    Calls thee to revel in her bliss ;
Nature but breathes one word, ' Rejoice ! '
    And Zephyr hails thee with a kiss.

IX

Ah ! what is sweeter in this life
    Than a fair breezy day in June,
When rippling brooks in mimic strife
    Purl lazily a sleepy tune ?

X

Whilst reeds in gentle music bend,
    And call on Syrinx as they sigh,
In notes as sweet as Pan might send
    From reed-pipe in the days gone by.

XI

O Phyllis, come ! Each wind-waved leaf
    Can its own love-lorn tale relate ;
The pine-trees bow in faithful grief,
    And mourn o'er Pithys' hapless fate.

XII

And wood and mountain, wind and stream,
  Of many an old-world legend tell,
When mortals lived in golden dream,
  And gods did on Olympus dwell.

XIII

Whilst over hill, through dale, through grove,
  Shall Echo, with immortal tongue,
Wail how Narcissus scorned her love,
  And o'er the flood enchanted hung.

XIV

O Phyllis, come! Sweet mistress, hear!
  Thy presence makes the earth divine ;
Take from my heart its love-born fear,
  Lest Echo's hapless fate be mine.

DAPHNE.

RARE eyes that make a twofold sun
   Upon the world to shine,
Red lips that turn the ruby dull,
   A face and form divine ;
A footstep fleet as that of fawn,
A blush as bright as rosy dawn,
   My Daphne, all are thine.

But ah ! why should that glorious sun
   For me o'erclouded be ;
The lips that answer others' jests
   Ne'er give one smile to me ?
Why should morn's flush grow dark as night,
And oft when I appear in sight,
   My Daphne fail to see ?

In vain I twine a garland fair,
    The flowers she flings away ;
In vain my verse breathes fond conceits,
    She scorns each tender lay.
And if I whisper words of love,
And swear by all the stars above,
    My Daphne—goes away.

Yet still my harp is tuned to sing
    Of Daphne, spite of scorn,
Since the most perfect joy I have
    Is from sweet Daphne drawn.
If she despise the love I bear,
No willow-wreath be mine to wear,
    Though slighted love I mourn :

Apollo-like, my brows I'll crown
    Through her most sweet disdain
With laurel, for my constant song
    Of Daphne fame shall gain ;
For Daphne keeps my heart, and I
Am captive, with no heart to fly,
    No wish to break my chain.

FAIR MELISSA.

FAIR MELISSA through the grove
   Listlessly was straying,
Thinking of her absent love
   Promised tryst delaying.
' Fair is false, and false is fair,
Men are traitors everywhere!'
   Quoth Melissa, sighing.

Tripping came a little maid—
   ' Maiden, where dost wander ? '
' But to find the crock of gold,
   Where the bow stoops yonder.'
' Fair is false, and false is fair,
Hope deceives us everywhere ! '
   Quoth Melissa, sighing.

Next drew nigh a pensive youth—
  ' Whither art thou hieing ? '
' Lady fair, to search for Truth
  In the dark well lying.'
' Fair is false, and false is fair ;
Truth, she dwells not anywhere ! '
  Quoth Melissa, sighing.

Plucked she roses from the hedge ;
  But a thorn among them,
Hidden, tore her dainty skin—
  Quick away she flung them.
' Fair is false, and false is fair,
Beauty is a cruel snare,'
  Quoth Melissa, sighing.

Lo ! an arm around her thrown,
  Lo ! a deep voice pleading ;
Whilst soft kisses on her hand
  Stop the wound from bleeding.
Doubts and fears flee fast away,
' Hope, Truth, Love, I've found to-day ! '
  Quoth she—without sighing.

WOOING.

THROUGH the meadows, nigh the hedge-row,
With the May-snow silver-laden,
Whence doth sweet spring incense rise,
There I met a blooming maiden:
'Maiden, thou hast won a prize;
Lost to me are both mine eyes;
Ere I saw thee, they could see
All fair sights on earth that be;
Now they only mirror thee;
Take them; yet, it thou would'st give
In exchange one glance so kind,
I would be content to live
For ever blind.'
'What are thy two eyes to me?'
Lightly laughing, spake the maid;
'Since I see, without their aid,
Flatterers ever men will be.'

Through the meadows in the summer,
Flushed the hedge-rows all with roses,
. There the maid again I found
Culling fairest buds for posies.
' Maiden, thou my tongue hast bound ;
Once it sang of all around,
Now it is but moved to sing,
" Love came by on idle wing,
Aimed a dart and left a sting."
Take my speech, yet for love's sake,
One sweet word of pity give,
That may me contented make
Aye dumb to live.'
Lightly laughed the maiden then,
' Worthless is thy speech to me,
False for ever it must be,
Since so false the hearts of men.'

Through the cornfields in the autumn,
When the sheaves stood ripe and golden,
There the maid once more I met ;
Sorrow did my soul embolden ;
' Maid, thou art on mischief set,
Thou hast proved a worse thief yet ;

Thou hast stol'n my heart away,
Give it back.'   But she said, 'Nay,
What I win is mine alway.'
Blush'd she like the rose in June,
Turn'd she as the lily pale,
Soft her voice, like murmuring tune
Of summer gale.
' We are quits—the game is played;
If thy heart's no longer thine,
Truly thou hast taken mine,
And art therefore fairly paid.'

THE SONG.

I HEARD a song in the morning,
  Ere ever the birds awoke ;
It rose as the waves on the pebbles
  In splinters of silver broke ;
It came with the burst of music
  The babbling rivulet played ;
It came with the hum of a thousand notes
  The gossamer insects made ;
It came with the leaf-stirring breezes,
  It sprang from each opening flower ;
It echoed from hill to valley,
  It dripped in each summer shower.
And I listened and listened—such music
  I never had heard before,
And I felt I could lie and listen
  To its sweetness for evermore.

I heard it again at noonday,
  As the mower whistled a tune ;
I heard it in every pulse that stirred
  Through the outer world in June,
For everything seemed alive with sound,
  Its melody round me to fling ;
I could hear the thistle-down whirling by,
  And the waft of the butterfly's wing ;
It chimed with the children's merry laugh
  As they sauntered home from school ;
It rushed with the roar that the mill-wheel made
  As it splashed in the quiet pool ;
It sounded clear as the village clock
  Struck briskly the mid-day hour ;
And it swung from the bells as the ringers rang
  In the time-worn belfry tower ;
Or ever they rang the joy-bell peal,
  Or ever the death-bell tolled ;
Yet still I heard it—a living song,
  That would never grow dead and cold.

I told it at eve to my darling,
  And my darling looked gravely at me ;
Quoth she, ' The song that I care for
  Another song must be ;

And thou, if thou truly didst love me,
    A sweeter song would'st have heard
Than ever was whispered by breezes
    Or ever was sung by bird.'

I listened again at midnight,
    When the world was all asleep ;
And lo ! a lovelier song I heard
    Throughout the silence sweep.
I felt my heart-chords stirring ;
    Beside me there was none ;
I knew what my darling cared for
    As I heard each tender tone.
'O love ! O love ! this music
    Comes from my heart alone.'

THE SPOILER DESPOILED.

MUSING in the autumn twilight, lulled by the low
    droning wind,
That doth strangely stir the cobwebs in the store-
    rooms of my mind ;
Sweeping them from mouldering pictures that have
    lain forgotten there,
Freshening up the quaint old framework till it seemeth
    passing fair ;
To each picture whispering stories of the deeds of
    long ago,
Each a parable foretelling truths in time I came to
    know,
But whose meaning passed unheeded as I looked
    with childish eyes
On the world outstretched before me in its blooming
    Eden guise ;

When there was no Past, no Future, all my being
    seemed to cling
To a world that was the Present, circled by a fairy
    ring,
Watered by another river flowing through a land of
    gold,
Compassing as fair a country as Havilah's stream of old.
Ah! that glorious dream-life season never will return
    to me,
Ne'er with eyes undimmed, unfearing, springtide I
    again shall see,
For a rude hand grasped my treasure, and a rude
    voice seemed to say,
'All the sweet beliefs of childhood harder creeds
    shall sweep away.'
Yet around their vanished beauty still a hallowed
    brightness lies,
Still as from long-faded roses, doth a lingering sweet-
    ness rise,
And I know that I have caught a fleeting glimpse of
    Paradise.
Oh! that golden age that memory traces in Hesperian
    prime,
Like to some rare ancient painting mellowed by the
    hand of Time;

When the cherry-tree seemed laden with a freight of
　　fairy snow,
And the blushing apple-blossoms set the orchard all
　　aglow ;
When the waxen-flowered syringa peeped above the
　　garden walls,
And the lilac matched its clusters 'gainst the guelder-
　　rose's balls ;
When I half believed the river was some wild en-
　　chanted tide,
And at moonlight on its waters elfin fleets were seen
　　to glide—
River winding through the sedges 'neath the bending
　　willow-trees,
Sparkling, glinting in the sunlight, rippled by the
　　perfumed breeze ;
Creeping through the clover meadows, through the
　　thyme-sweet valleys borne,
Where the poppy plants its banner scarlet-bright
　　among the corn ;
Narrowing, deepening, darker growing as it steals its
　　onward way,
Through the woods where I have spent full many a
　　merry holiday ;

H

When the leaves were turning yellow, when the nuts
    were ruddy brown ;
Or when Spring, with budding blossom, wandered
    forth the woods to crown ;
When each bird from bush and bramble gaily carolled
    to its mate,
Little dreaming thoughtless boyhood meant its home
    to desolate ;
When amidst the swaying branches cooed the dove
    in murmurs soft,
And the rook's hoarse note resounded from his rocking
    home aloft ;
Blackbird, thrush, or skilful chaffinch with its lichen-
    spangled nest,
Wren, or graceful water-wagtail, each the object of
    my quest—
Through the fields, adown the fallows where peewits
    and corncrakes hide,
Or by reedy streams whereon the water-hens so
    proudly glide ;
Like a warrior carrying warfare into some fair peace-
    ful land,
All intent upon the booty tempting my too eager
    hand,

Forth I wandered, little heeding days of ceaseless
    patient toil

That had formed the curious structure destined soon
    to be my spoil ;

Little recked of birds made homeless, little recked of
    wrong or right,

All the wrong had faded, vanished, in the blaze of
    glory's light.

Boyhood e'en has its ambition ; I was brave, and lithe,
    and young,

And I felt my blood all glowing as from bough to
    bough I swung ;

Up the gnarled old oak I clambered, up its dizzy
    height I scaled,

Never once my foothold faltered, never once my spirit
    failed ;

Dauntless then I seized the treasure, proudly bore it
    to the ground.

But another claimant met me, angrily on me he
    frowned ;

He had marked the nest, and therefore held it as his
    lawful prize,

Should he now submit to see it carried off before his
    eyes ?

I had stolen a march upon him, I my booty must
    resign ;
I was strong, but he was stronger, and the battle was
    not mine.

.   .   .   .   .   .

So I went indignant homeward, homeward went with-
    out my nest,
And I sobbed out all my wrongs and anger on my
    mother's breast.
Gently then she soothed me, bade me learn a lesson
    from my woe :
' Thus, my child, thou'lt ever find it when the world
    thou com'st to know :
Might is right the whole earth over, this much thou
    canst understand,
And the strong ones o'er the weak ones aye will have
    the upper hand.
Thou didst rob the birds, my darling, for thy might
    seemed right to thee,
Then in turn there came a stronger, spoiler of thy
    spoil to be.
He avenged the birds unjustly, yet the moral thou
    mayst read ;
E'en in this life retribution follows every wrongful
    deed.'

THE LOST FLOWER.

A MAIDEN threw a flower into the stream,
　　It floated—whither?
Kissed by the west wind, gilded by the gleam
Of flaming sun, and silvered by the beam
　　Of the pale moon,
All gold and ivory inwrought with pearl it seemed,
And incensed with a sweeter fragrance.　Soon
　Upon the flower she doated:
‘ O waters, turn your tide, my flower bear hither!’
　But still away it floated:
　　Whither, whither?

The rippling waters sang in ceaseless song,
　　‘Whither, ah, whither?’
The sun went down, the west wind swept along,
The moon was hidden dark night clouds among;
　　And lost to sight

The flower. The maiden with strange yearning longed
To lure the blossom back, now grown so bright,
   And more on it she doated,
Crying, ' O wind, O wind, my flower waft hither ! '
   Yet still it onward floated :
     Whither, whither ?

The maiden, weeping, watched upon the shore,
   Still sighing, ' Whither ? '
Perhaps the morning light may joy restore :
Nay, what is lost is lost for evermore.
   Mortals, be wise :
No treasure flung away can be restored.
The sun moves forward in the trackless skies,
   And golden opportunity,
Once gone, returns not hither,
   And the great flood of teeming life rolls by :
     Whither, ah, whither ?

SPINNING.

SPINNING a slender flaxen thread
  That sudden is snapped in twain ;
Dreaming over an idle dream
  Whose sweetness is lost in pain ;
Spinning and dreaming from morn to eve,
  Is all the dreaming in vain ?

White-winged butterflies flitting among
  . The golden bloom of the grass,
Red moss-roses with rich perfume,
  That the light winds kiss and pass ;
April sunshine, then April cloud,
And a sad heart sighing 'Alas!'

Spinning, spinning a tangled thread
  With many a break and join,
Many a fret and many a knot

Spun to one complex line :
It takes a knotted and much-pieced thread
  To weave out the life divine.

Royal white lilies in chaliced pearl,
  Gathering the dews of heaven ;
Glorious trail of shining stars,
  Over the dark night driven;
A fountain with bubbling crystal wave,
  And a golden bowl that's riven.

The sun glints in through the twining vine,
  And the bird sings on the bough ;
The spinner hears but one heart-struck chord,
  And the sun is darkened now ;
She spins and dreams o'er the broken thread
  A dream of a broken vow.

NOT LOST.

THE sun dropped down, the crescent moon
   Went slowly sailing by,
All in the burning chrysoprase
   Of the sultry summer sky,
That crowned the crimson-banded west
   With blue and amber dye.

The twilight grey rose up a-near
   Each shining golden horn ;
And twinkled one by one the stars
   Over the yellow corn ;
And dimmer grew the silver flush
   Of the daisies on the lawn.

Yet high above the moon and stars,
   The maiden raised her eyes ;
' Not on this earth, but in thine heaven,

O Lord, my treasure lies ;
Grant me one glimpse behind the veil
   That hides Thy paradise ! '

And greyer grew the summer night,
   As sleep sweet mocked the dead ;
And whiter fell the white moon rays
   Upon the maiden's bed ;
And lo, an angel stooped and kissed
   The tears she dreaming shed.

Her grief-stained eyelids softly touched
   And the mist-veil was riven,
And past the stars her soul was borne,
   Through the night-hush to Heaven.
'Among God's shining ones,' she said,
   To him a place is given.'

She sought throughout the glorious streets,
   Yet found of him no trace ;
'Among thy blessèd ones, O Lord !
   Hath my dead love no place ? '
And down, a-down, her fainting soul
   Sank through the golden space.

' Why weepest thou ?   God's angels walk
  The earth on errand sent.'
She turned her at the voice and gazed
  In joyful wonderment ;
' Art thou so near although unseen ?
  Then is my soul content.'

The reddening dawn stole slowly on,
  The sun rose up.   The moon
Turned into silver ; and the maid
  Said, ' I have waked too soon.'
Yet through the day she smiled, for still
  At morn, at eve, at noon,
There walked an angel at her side—
  ' Lord ! I shall see him soon.'

A LEGEND OF ST. CECILIA.

I

FROM heaven's half-open portals swept
In diapason rare,
That trembled through the air,
The murmur of the angel quire;
So sweet that Nature listening wept,
And, filled with fond desire,
Caught up the falling silver notes
And prisoned them in summer breeze,
Or tinted cloud that idly floats
To burst in rain-drops 'mongst the trees;
Or flung them in the heaving tide
That laves the purple isles in June,
Or cast them on the mountain side
To quiver out their tune;
Till earth is filled with heavenly sound,
Heaven's speech, sweet music hovers round.

II

Nor Nature heard alone
The immortal strain ;
Deep in man's heart each seraph tone
Found a refrain,
Awaked from chords that erst all mute had lain ;
In wild delicious swell
The new-born sense
Of beauty grew to rapture so intense
That the pulse rose and fell
In throes sublime ;
Man panted to reveal the song
So God-like in his soul upstirred,
A God-like gift to after-time,
Celestial words through ages long :
And fierce he strove, until were heard
The passionate throbs of melody forth wrung
From surcharged heart, all heaven-enthralled ;
And in entrancing pain
Did he an utterance gain,
And in that utterance was Musician called.

III

E'en so the holy maid Cecilia
In adoration hung
On the celestial notes escaping
As heaven's gate open swung ;
She, soul-inspired, like Echo clear
Perfect repeats each glorious tone,
And wondering seraphs pause to hear
A voice so like their own :
Through starlight night
They wing their flight,
And earthward bringing
The breath of heaven, listen with pure delight
To her melodious singing ;
And round her gathering, incite
The mellow notes to more divine outpouring,
To which men hearken in amaze,
And the fair marvel praise ;
While upward soaring
Angels rejoice
That mortal voice
So sweet unto the earth is given
As to draw down the hosts of heaven.

IV

And thus it chanced,
The angels whispering as she sang entranced,
(Unconscious if in heaven, or if she dreamed)
Bade her ' Behold.'   And lo ! a shining place
Wherein there gleamed
Great pipes of gold, that drank apace
All sound.   Filling their golden throats
With precious winds that blew from Paradise ;
And straight arise
In purest harmony strange solemn notes ;
Such awe-inspiring tones that ne'er before
Issued from instrument of man's devising ;
Swelling in deepening wrath like thunder roar,
Or jubilant with praise uprising :
Now pleading like sad angel hearts that roam
The earth, and weep for blinded man astray ;
Bringing repentance and the trespass home,
That through the sweet reproof men kneel and pray
With low bowed heads ; for they the voice divine
Have heard through gorgeous music in their souls,
Yet tempered with quick mercy that doth shine
Resplendent as the music softer rolls

In dying dulcet waves, that mounting higher
Sound like the far-off chime of cherub-quire.

V

Cecilia kept the vision in her heart
As revelation of His holy will,
Who to His chosen great ones doth impart
The work they must fulfil ;
Until in time
Through vast cathedral aisles rolled forth sublime
From organ golden-piped so rare a flood
Of melody, that men with one accord
All reverent stood,
Saying, 'Praise we the Lord.'

MY NEIGHBOUR'S DAUGHTER.

My good old neighbour hath a little daughter,
Fair as the lily-bud, sweet as the rose;
Sunny is her hair as the golden summer,
White is her brow as the winter snows:
Gaily she smiles as she passes by me,
Never a grief or a care she knows.

Pleasant is the voice of my neighbour's daughter,
Soft as the woodquest's, sighing as the breeze,
Ringing like plash of far-off silver waters,
Rippling like rustle of leaf-stirred trees;
Men idly listening, with senses half dreaming,
Wake into lovers at sounds like these.

Down to the river steals my neighbour's daughter,
Where droops the willow its boughs in the tide,
Where the lithe water-flags their gay heads upraising,

I

Mark out a creek where a boat may glide.
Not all alone is my neighbour's daughter,
Some one by the river lingers at her side.

Through summer days, when the scarlet fruit is rip'n
    ing,
Flushes her fair cheek with deeper hue ;
Through summer days, when sapphire skies are smiling
Laugh the maiden's eyes with a tenderer blue ;
Through summer midnights lies she still a-dreaming,
Dreaming bright dreams that at morning prove true.

A tell-tale face hath my neighbour's daughter,
Betraying the secret she fancies to keep :
' Nay, maiden, nay ! thorns ever come with roses—
Eyes that shine brightly must sometimes weep.
Where the sun glows with a wonderful splendour,
Sharpest cut shadows will darkest creep.'

Trusting is the heart of my neighbour's daughter :
' Nay, he will never be false to me.'
Day after day she awaits his returning
Down by the river that winds to the sea ;
Yet sad is the heart of my neighbour's daughter,
White grow her cheeks as the snow on the lea.

Dark grows her life as the cloud skies at even,
Cold grows her heart as the ice-bound lake:
'Nay, he will never be false' still she whispers,
Whispers with heart that is ready to break.
Fain would I comfort my neighbour's daughter—
'Maiden, in springtide dead hopes to life awake.'

Through summer woods the summer birds are singing,
Butterflies have plumed their wings, and flowers are
　　　　blooming fair ;
Down to the river steals my neighbour's little daughter
Water-flags wave gaily, a boat waits there;
Glides she so shyly with the shimmering sunlight
Fresh gold lending to her golden hair.

Through summer woods the summer birds are singing,
To her beating heart what notes of joy they speak !
Hath the summer wind set her sweet face a-glowing ?
Hath the golden summer brought back roses to her
　　　　cheek ?
Nay, but a voice, than bird or breezes sweeter,
Hath whispered back the roses by the yellow-bannered
　　　　creek.

THE TWO SISTERS.

Two hearts were full of joy at morn,
  At eve one wailed,
'Ah! would that I had ne'er been born,'
  And wept and sighed from night to dawn
    While the stars paled ;
  And crimson-crowned through mists of gray
  Flushed into life the glorious day.
      Ah, well-a-day! Ah, well-a-day!
      So pine forsaken hearts away.

The other wreathed her brow around
  With buds of spring,
Sweet primroses with violets bound.
Her voice with tender flute-like sound
  Went murmuring,
'O life fair as a summer sea
Gently thy waves break over me.'
      Ah, well-a-day! Ah, well-a-day!
      So full some hearts of joy alway.

Nay,' quoth the first, 'the breakers roar
  With ceaseless moan,
The sea-fogs hide the longed-for shore,
The haven will be neared no more :
    Alone! alone!
And all is dark, the moon on high
Is hidden as the storm sweeps by.'
      Ah, well-a-day! Ah, well-a-day!
      So from some hearts light fades away.

The dazzling sun the other caught
  Into her eyes ;
It shimmer'd o'er her hair and brought
A radiance round her, all inwrought
  With thousand dyes.
'O light,' she cried, ' about my soul
Like an eternal aureole.'
      Ah, well-a-day! Ah, well-a-day!
      In some hearts sunshine dwells alway.

' Nay,' quoth the first, 'the sun hath set
  In the lone west.
My cheeks with heavy tears are wet,
In vain my heart strives to forget
  And find a rest.

My love is false, my heart forlorn,
Oh would that I had ne'er been born.'
    Ah, well-a-day! Ah, well-a-day!
    Some hearts must bleed on earth alway.

The other sang, 'There is no night;
    Midsummer-tide
Reigns through the world with love-fires bright.
A fairy-land rose-bathed in light:
    By river-side
Forget-me-nots with blossoms blue
And reeds soft whisper—He is true:'
    Ah, well-a-day! Ah, well-a-day!
    Some hearts 'mongst roses bloom alway.

So goes the world to this and this,
    From morn to morrow,
One life for woe, and one for bliss;
To some love's grief, to some love's kiss;
    Some joy—some sorrow—
The thread through each web must be spun
That breaks not until life is done.
    Ah, well-a-day! Ah, well-a-day!
    The death-sleep calms all grief away.

Passed by a shadow as dark as night
  Earth's brightness o'er ;
Passed by a seraph robed in light
Blotting the darkness out of sight,
  And evermore
Another star from heaven doth shine,
An earth-voice chants in quires divine.
    Ah, well-a-day ! Ah, well-a-day !
    So may we wake to joy some day.

HEIDELBERG, AUGUST 7, 1867.[1]

(IN MEMORIAM.)

A DAY of smiles and tears, half cloud, half sunshine,
And then the heavens cast away their frown,
And, in their rarest garb of dazzling beauty,
On Heidelberg looked down.

The setting sun bathed in a flood of amber
Each tower and buttress of the castle old,
And loving rays tinged carven scrolls and tracery
With ruddy tints of gold.

[1] At the close of the summer term it is customary for the students
of Heidelberg to indulge in various acts of rejoicing. A favourite one
appears to be going in procession to Neckarsteinach, and returning
from thence in the evening in a barge decorated with lamps or lights of
different kinds. From this barge, or from a smaller boat accompanying
it, rockets and other fireworks are let off, producing a very beautiful
effect as the boat comes slowly down in the darkness. Sometimes the
bridge is illuminated with Bengal fire, and occasionally, as in the
present instance, the castle is also lighted up. On the occasion al-
luded to in the verses, the 'Vandalia' corps, its numbers being in-
creased by the 'Vandalen' from all parts of Germany, delighted the

And in the sapphire sky a rainbow, glowing
With fairest colours, softly died away
As twilight, wrapped in misty robe, descended
To chase the fading day.

And twilight mellowed down the clear cut edges
That fringing tree-tops traced against the sky ;
And through white rifts of clouds the moon was
      beaming,
Faint stars peeped forth on high.

And lights along the river bank were glancing
In yellow gleams athwart fair Neckar's tide,
And underneath the bridge's shadowy arches
The rippled waters sighed.

Heidelberger population with a spectacle of great beauty. From a
house on the Neuenheim side of the river, close by the bridge and
immediately opposite the 'Corpskneipe' of the Vandalen, which was
at one time brilliantly illuminated, I probably witnessed one of the
loveliest sights I shall ever behold. The house commanded a view of
the whole line of proceedings. From the mountain behind it, the
torch procession started to meet the boat coming down the river, and,
then marching parallel with it, crossed the bridge just as the boat
reached it. Opposite to me, the castle towered over the light-dotted
town ; whilst at my feet flowed the dark river, with the streams of light
flashing across its waters ; and the moon, when she looked out from
behind the clouds, turning into silver its lines of ripples. The effect of
the various lights as the castle rose out of the darkness is beyond de-
scription.

And with their murmur pealing bells were chiming
A melody, as though some spirit hand had dashed
Deep sounding chords on rare Eolian harp-strings,
Or silver cymbals clashed.

The signal gun, from hill to hill resounding,
Is heard.   And ever darker grows the night ;
And o'er the mountain path flame out the torches,
Tracking the way in light.

March on, march on ; the fiery boat advances,
Ablaze with golden spray and glittering star,
And brilliant streams across the clear night heavens
The rockets shoot afar.

And midst the shower of fire the student chorus,
' *Frei ist der Bursch*,' doth o'er the waters float,
Then changing—to the old field-marshal's glory
Bursts forth the warlike note.[1]

And o'er the bridge the student band moves onward,
With waving torches and with banners gay,
Whilst slow the student barge, through fire-lit arches
Glides on its glittering way.

[1] ' *Was blasen die Trompeten*,' in honour of Blucher.

But hark ! a startling peal like crashing thunder,
And in an instant, from the shades of night,
Like gorgeous fairy scene, in magic beauty
The castle sprang to light.

Wrapped its old towers and walls in flames of crimson,
Whilst at its foot a cloud of emerald rolled,
And bright shone out each pinnacle and turret,
All tipped with burnished gold ;

As if some elfin troop in wayward humour
Had turned the crumbling stones to gems full rare,
Or caught some falling star midway from heaven
And held it shining there.

The rosy rays upon the waters glancing
Lit like to ruby wine the waves below,
And the cold brow and cheek of stately Pallas
Flushed with a deeper glow,

As calmly watching o'er her favoured city
She on her students' joy-time gazed with pride,
Whilst clearer rang the song, and brighter flashing
Flowed Neckar's crimson tide.

Hail, Heidelberger students!   In your springtide
Of golden student life, so fresh, so free.
A summer dream, bright with a long past sunshine,
In graver years to be.

Yet for that future, brave true hearts up-raising,
All honour then to caps of every hue ;
Hail to the ' Schwaben ' with their gleaming yellow,
The red!   the green! the blue!

Hail to the ' Preussen ' with their death-earned colours,
In freedom's cause may they march proudly on,
And bear to victory unstained, unsullied,
The flag their fathers won.

All hail to the ' Vandalen's ' brighter banner!
Long may it float above the castled Rhine!
O'er hearts that in their country's wreath of glory
Fresh laurels shall entwine.

O lovely Heidelberg!   O town enchanted!
How many a memory fondly to thee clings!
How many a poet-hand hath struck in rapture
For thee the silver strings.

Fain would I fling thee one fair flower at parting
If but the power to cull that flower were mine,
And to thy welfare drain the '*Abschied*' goblet,
Brimming with sparkling wine.

Alas! bright dreams bring sorrowful awaking ;
In every life comes many a sad farewell ;
Farewell! yet ever on my heart engraven
Wilt thou in beauty dwell.

Farewell Vandalen! Ne'er to be forgotten ;
Still as I float adown Time's rapid tide,
Oft shall your pageant in unfading colours
From Memory's portal glide.

ON AN OFFER OF MARRIAGE WRITTEN TO ' MISTRESS MARTHA —— ' AUGUST 30, 1729.

A TIME-STAINED letter, in stiff-pointed hand
Writ nigh a century and half ago,
An offer—worded in respectful style,
Pleading for ' Ay,' and yet half fearing ' No ; '
A quaint short letter full of courteous phrase,
In fashion in the Second George's days.

Writ early in the Second George's days
When swords were drawn and sounds of war were rife :
' Dear Madam,' it begins, then further on
He courage takes, ' dear Patty, be my wife.'
Far sweeter music breathing from his pen
Than the ' Te Deum ' sung for Dettingen.

He in the town, with London sights agape,
Found nought that pleased him, for his heart had fled

Into the pleasant country far away,
Dreaming how time with gentle Patty sped ;
Finding how day by day his love still grew
Until his heart poured forth its passion true.

How long the days ; how slow the weary nights ;
How dull the vapid pleasures of the town ;
How lone and lifeless all the crowded streets ;
How vain in fashion's whirl his thoughts to drown ;
'Court-pleasures,' so he wrote, 'I fain would flee
To be for ever, Patty dear, with thee.'

And what was Patty like ? One conjures up
The portrait of a youthful maiden fair,
Sweet, dignified, half dimpling into smiles,
And yet with somewhat serious in her air ;
As though some thought she did not care to speak
Had brought a deeper colour to her cheek.

It was the last of summer, in the time
That reapers gather in the yellow grain ;
When mellow August lays a golden hand
Upon the purple hills and verdant plain ;
When the coy breezes fitful kisses blow
And set the crimson hollyhocks all a-glow.

The last of summer.   But a summer new
Woke with the letter, in fair Patty's breast,
A summer that no fading blossoms owned ;
No storms, no blight, a halcyon season blest,
Born of the earnest prayer her lover made,
' Dear Patty, trust me.   Do not be afraid.'

The wafer and the rent her fingers made,
As trembling she the letter open tore,
May yet be seen upon the yellow page,
Whilst she who trembling oped it is no more.
The simple record of their hopeful life
Outlives a century the man and wife.

Thought wanders back through the dim vale of years
To that past summer time when roses seemed
To breathe from Paradise.   And heaven's wind stirred
A depth of melody that scarce she deemed
Belonged to earth, until the shaft of Love
Soft wounding taught her soul to soar above.

One tries to paint the courtship as it sped
In statelier wise than is the fashion now ;
' Madam, your humble lover,' and then makes,

Like Sir Charles Grandison, a reverent bow.
Thus he; whilst she with beating heart, in vain
A calm unruffled mien strives to maintain.

One falls to musing o'er the wedding-day,
And what was Mistress Patty's wedding-gown ;
A sacque of paduasoy, or broidered train,
Or riding habit ?   Was it made in town,
Or did some country mantua-maker's skill
Suffice th' important order to fulfil ?

Still through the distance ringing soft and clear
Comes the joy-peal of merry wedding-bell,
Waked up to sound through the dim-tinted page
That with the joy-bell blends the funeral knell :
For Death a black-draped banner hangs above
The date that ushers in the words of love.

Full nigh a century and half ago,
And 'neath the quiet turf the lovers lie ;
Children beside the grave have weeping stood
Who in their turn lay down in peace to die,
And children's children from the earth have passed,
Yet the love-letter has outlived the last.

K

Yes—such is life, wherein man plays his part—
A phantom drama—at the best a dream
Unreal, whilst to our earth-cumbered sense,
Meted by time, it doth most real seem :
Until the hand of Death the curtain rends
And the freed spirit to its home ascends.

A time-stained letter, in stiff pointed hand
Writ nigh a century 'and half ago ;
What is the charm that in its phrases lies
That over it one moralises so ?
'Tis this: the words to which our souls give birth
Are more immortal than our lives on earth.

LOVE AND SPRING.

SHAKING off the April drops
That her green robes spangle,
Spring trips blithesome o'er the flowers,
Heaped in glorious tangle.

Rainbow-crown and sun-gold rays
Into sainthood light her ;
Fresh-blown May-buds incense raise,
Clouded skies glow brighter.

Babbling brooks with silver tongues,
Birds in clear notes ringing,
' Spring is queen of all the earth,'
Through the woods are singing.

' Nay,' quoth Love, who listening lay
By the reed-bound river,
' Sweeter music I can wake,
Making heart-strings quiver.'

Whispered he throughout the land
Of a kingdom golden ;
Youth and maiden heard, and straight
In his chains were holden,

Spring half frowned ; Love smiling said,
' We two bring fair weather ; '
And since then, the poets say
They have reigned together.

JUNE.

FILL to my mistress the crystal cup!
Twine it with roses fair to see,
Foaming nectar all brimming up,
Such as the gods quaffed, fill for me!
The health I drink is a health divine
As long as the sun and stars shall be:
Hail to thee, June, sweet mistress mine!
Although thou hidest away from me.
In vain I wander throughout the land,
Close on the track of thy dainty feet,
Tracing the touch of thy gracious hand
On fruit and blossom and bending wheat.
I pass through the woods, and their deepened green
Tells me thy shadow hath fallen there,
And the rustling lime-trees say, ' She hath been,'
And flutter their flowers with a jaunty air;

While myriad blossoms in hedge-row and brake
Peep at me with their sleepy eyes,
And murmur, ' June kissed us all awake ;
But we cannot yet gaze at the dazzling skies.'
Soft as velvet beneath my feet—
Lo ! a rich carpet of green and gold,
Broidered with orchis and meadow-sweet,
And many a floweret I knew of old.
' How came ye hither, ye flowers, now say ? '
Quick out-spake the pimpernel bright :
' June sat weaving a web so gay,
All in the hush of the summer night.
June sat weaving a web last night,
Silver her threads in the moonlight seemed ;
But the sun flashed on them his glorious light,
And a thousand colours at day-dawn gleamed.'
I strolled through the fields of fragrant hay
Whilst the haymakers rested awhile at noon,
And as on the ground they idly lay,
Loud rang their praises of lovely June.
I turned to the farm-house so grey and old,
With its pointed roofs, and its straw-thatched sheds,
Its goodly cornstacks yellow as gold,
Its trim-kept garden with box-edged beds.

Wild at will grew the roses there,
Pinks filled the air with a rich perfume,
And I knew that June with a skill full rare
Had spangled the jasmine with starry bloom.
I wandered down to the shady pool,
And the waterflag's petals were all uncurled;
'Oh! waterflag by the waters cool,
Why is thy standard to-day unfurled?
Why sing the birds on bush and on tree?
Why so loud doth the grasshopper hum?'
And the waterflag gravely answered me,
'Because the Queen of the Year is come.'
O June! O June! sweet mistress mine!
Well may I drain the goblet to thee,
God-like nectar and golden wine,
Although thou hidest away from me.

I dreamed that I saw fair June last night,
And her eyes were dark as the violet,
Her robe was tinged with the emerald's light,
Her girdle with diamond dew-drops set.
Lilies and roses her fair brow crowned,
Lilies and roses twisted and twined;
Like a dark cloud floated her tresses unbound,
A dusky cloud with amber lined.

Softly she whispered, ' Be true as now,'
' True,' said I, ' To death will I be.'
Softly she kissed my burning brow,
And then the vision was lost to me.
   Night fled away and the morning rose,
And again fair June through the woods I seek,
And every waft of wind that blows
Brings back her kisses upon my cheek.
She's the fairest mistress that e'er I knew,
I've loved her many and many a day ;
And when age creeps on I will still be true,
Though my footstep falter, my locks turn grey.
And when in the grave forgotten I lie,
Sweet June will linger my grave to see ;
Perchance she may even breathe a sigh
And say, ' Ah ! why did such true love die ?
He was faithful unto me.'

JULY.

THROUGHOUT the house a dreamy stillness stole,
The watch-dog slept, scarce buzzed the lazy fly ;
The clock ticked on with solemn measured tone
Counting the drowsy moments of July.

Through quaint-shaped panes the mellow light crept in
And traced rare brown-gold shadows on the floor ;
The air was heavy with the scent that hung
Around the clematis that framed the door.

Through the clipped arches of the olden yew
I passed, and breathless silence reigned around ;
As though the earth by some enchanter's spell
In magic sleep were bound.

The peaches slumbered on the garden wall,
The dew upon their crimson cheeks was wet ;
The red-ripe strawberries gleamed amid their leaves
Like rubies in a ducal coronet.

The feathery wheat stood still as fairy spears
Borne by a million transfixed sentinels ;
The harebell was asleep, nor woke to ring
In honour of July her tiny bells.

The flame-tongued nightshade drooped her purple
          pride,
Yet held entranced the hedges where she clung ;
And wearied there, her trails of blossoms white
The wild convolvulus hung.

The river with its waveless waters lay
All motionless, as a pure crystal sea ;
Another landscape painted on the tide,
With spire, and sail, and tree.

Close by the rush-grown bank a boat was moored,
So still, it stirred not on the river's breast ;
The world was hushed, and Nature at my feet
Lay wrapped in perfect rest.

Like to the princess in the story old,
She in her beauty slept.   Oh sight of bliss !
Waiting until some poet-heart should come
And wake her with his kiss.

O wake ! O wake ! and breathe into my soul
Thy soul, that rightly I of thee may sing ;
Or—sleep for ever, in thy beauty veiled
'Neath July's wing.

OCTOBER.

CONQUEST-FLUSHED, like a warrior bold,
   On his mettlesome steed October brown,
   Over the hills, the valleys adown,
     Rideth ;
Trampling the rustling leaves of gold,
   As his steed he onward guideth.

At every tramp of his charger's hoof,
   He buries a treasure and mutters a charm,
   And the wandering wind a jubilant psalm
     Singeth ;
Whilst mischievous frost-sprites stand aloof,
   Nor harm the seed that he flingeth.

And the night-stars whisper to him who wakes
   A deeper meaning than dreamers can read,
   ' Life shall arise from the buried seed ;

Then know
That Death gives life for the life he takes,
　　As Nature doth forth-show.'

Over lakes and rivers he shakes his spear,
　And the angler stands where the river rolls past,
　And the purple mountains deep shadows cast
　　In the tide ;
And he sees far down in the water clear
　　The speckled troutlets glide.

Tramp through the orchard, each bough low bends,
　Laden with treasure October to greet,
　Eager its blushing wealth at his feet
　　To pour ;
For the kindly smile that on all he sends
　　Hath made him a king twice o'er.

Then when the fire crackles and logs bright blaze,
　And Hallowe'en nuts are burning slow,
　And mirrors to maidens their lovers show,
　　Fill up !
And drain to jolly October's praise,
　　In ale that he's kissed, a parting cup.

NOVEMBER.

I

Lo, a dim phantom steals across the land,
  Mist-shrouded, sad November,
Painting out leafless trees with shadowy hand,
And twining fog-wreaths round the old church-tower,
Whose deep-toned bell proclaims from hour to hour,
  ' O year, remember,
Thy life is nigh its close, so whispers chill November.'

II

The sky-lark's song, that heavenward did float,
  Dies before sad November ;
Hushed by the silent pool the frog's harsh note,
And summer birds are gone ; and in his nest
The sleeping squirrel takes his winter rest,
  And doth remember
The summer in his dreams, nor cares for drear
    November.

III

He dreams, nor wakes up at the cheery sounds
  That startle grim November,
The huntsman's horn, the eager baying hounds,
The tramp of horse's hoofs, the view halloo,
As wily Reynard flees before the crew,
  Nor doth remember
The cunning feints he made to cheat them last
    November.

IV

Scared by the jovial shouts, with frowning brow,
  Creeps onward dark November ;
And cities vast are shadow-cities now,
With spectre-lamps all sickly-glaring lit,
Whilst through the shadow-streets dim torches flit,
  And men remember,
And mingle Eastern myths and genii with November.

V

Half mist, half sunshine, fitful is the reign
  Of ghost-like, sad November ;
Like to a human life, half joy, half pain,

Reality and shadow blent together,
Storm, calm, and summer-gleam 'midst wintry weather
    As men remember
The chequered lights and shades of many a past
        November.

NEW YEAR'S DAY.

PEAL, peal from the belfry tower,
The bells are ringing at midnight :
  The ringers ring a joyous chime,
  'A child is born to Father Time,'
And the bells ring out at midnight.

Brave hearts are listening in the town,
For the first soft chime at midnight,
  And the shout goes up, 'Hail, New Year, hail !
  Bring strength and courage that ne'er shall fail,
To carry us through earth's midnight.'

As for the angel's step in the pool,
So the watchers watch at midnight,
  Loving women waiting to pray
  For blessings on those who are far away,
When the bells ring out at midnight.

L

A ship is nearing the harbour bar,
The beacon light flashes at midnight,
  And the bells ring merrily over the sea,
  'Sailor, a double welcome to thee,
The New Year is born this midnight.'

The ringers ring with a lusty will,
And the voice goes forth at midnight,
  'A brave New Year, a happy year
  To old and young, all people hear—
Bless ye the bells at midnight.

'Bless ye the bells, for angel hands
Have tuned their notes at midnight,
  That so to every heart their voice
  Shall sound, "The New Year's come, rejoice,
God's gift to us this midnight."'

THE BURIAL OF THE OLD YEAR.

I

I DUG a grave at midnight, there to bury
  A sorrow-stricken, bent, and wounded form ;
'Old friend,' quoth I, 'we've roughed the world to-
      gether,
  Through sunshine and through storm.

II

'Take with thee to thy rest my sins, my sorrows,
  My wrongs, my hopes, all blurred with bitter tears ;
Let them lie silent in thy breast for ever,
  Nor darken coming years.'

III

Beside the grave there stood an angel-watcher ;
  'Nay, for their work is yet undone,' spake he ;
'They must live on to teach thee truths learned only
  Through long heart-agony.'

IV

Next cast I in the grave joys gone for ever,
  Love, noble impulses, and god-like thought,
Lest that the longing after bright days faded
  Should be to madness wrought.

V

' Bury them not,' outspake the angel-watcher,
  ' No noble deed but bears fruit manifold ;
No act of love but lives, though unrequited ;
  No truth but keeps its hold.

VI

' Bury them not ! When wilder storms are raging,
  When darker clouds on thy horizon rise,
Like beacon lights through Time's touch clearer
    growing,
  Shall shine their memories.'

VII

Then turned I to the grave I dug at midnight,
  Where pale and cold in death the Old Year slept ;
And bending down I kissed his forehead lightly,
  And bitterly I wept.

VIII

'Old friend,' quoth I, 'we part to-night for ever,
  And I must bear the burden thou hast borne,
Until I hear the whispered words from heaven,
  " Blessèd are they that mourn."'

IX

' Blessèd, thrice blessèd they,' a voice made answer,
  And at that voice sweet bells began to ring,
Clear from a thousand belfry turrets pealing,
  To hail the New Year king.

X

The New Year king, like to a fair child-angel,
  Pressed down the sods upon the Old Year's grave,
And lo, rare amaranth flowers of heavenly beauty
  All glorious o'er it wave.

XI

He plucked one flower, and in his bosom laid it ;
  ' Thus in the present aye shall live the past,
No grief, no joy, no hope the Old Year cherished
  Shall to the winds be cast.'

XII

He stood there like the Resurrection-angel,
  Conquering the flesh through spiritual strife,
And I beheld the Old Year in the Present
  Raised to immortal life.

XIII

He stood, his flaming sword still pointing onward;
  My grief was hushed, and faith o'ercame each fear
I blessed the Old Year in his dark grave sleeping,
  And hailed the New-born Year.

YESTERDAY.

THE birds are darting on joyous wing,
The wind a tune o'er the hills is blowing,
The stream in dreamy music is flowing,
And yet I cannot sing ;
My lips are still on this summer day,
My heart is cold, and a shadow gray
Points ever backward to Yesterday.

Dripped through the branches the thunder-rain,
Hushed were the birds, and ever my weeping
Measure with Summer's hot pulse was keeping
In passionate refrain.
Then laughed the sun through the cloudlets gay,
But the pain in my heart died not away,
And the shadow pointed to Yesterday.

The west was glowing with purple bars,
The golden sun was lost in the river,
The moon shone out, and a silver quiver
Of light fell over the stars ;
And living murmurs all died away ;
Yet close beside me the shadow gray
Evermore pointed to Yesterday.

Faded the stars, and the dawning red
Over the distant hills was stealing,
And softly the village bells were pealing
A chime as for the dead !
And morning and night and bright noon-day
To the past still bore my thoughts away,
Till each to-morrow seemed Yesterday.

Past, weary past ! wilt thou never die ?
Say, shall there nevermore come a morrow
Lighted by hope and untouched by sorrow ?
Sudden athwart the sky
Arching over the storm-clouds gray
Flashed sun-painted a rainbow gay
Paling the darkness of Yesterday.

Gleamed with pure storm-pearls the bridge divine,
And the wild soul waters ceased their sobbing,
And hushed was my heart's fierce fever throbbing
At sight of the holy sign ;
The haunting shadow vanished away,
And I seemed to hear the angels say,
' The Future is born of Yesterday.'

'MEMENTO DOMINE.'

AT midnight went a cry throughout the land,
Swift the Death-Angel flew on mighty wings ;
Lo ! he hath smitten with relentless hand
   The palaces of kings.

At morning rose a wild and wailing cry,
' Mourn for the great, the good, in death laid low.'
And England prostrate in her grief doth lie—
   ' " *Memento Domine*," a nation's woe.'

Through stone-wrought tracery, in painted rays
The sunlight falls on carvings rare and quaint,
Where, 'neath groined roof the sinner kneels and prays
   Nigh sculptured saint.

Hushed is the organ now—through aisle so dim
Sadly resounds the solemn litany—
Be still each heart ! No prayer is heard for *him*,
   But—' *Miserere nobis Domine.*'

'Neath plainer roofs void of adorning grace,
Whence many a heartfelt prayer to Heaven's upborne,
Sorrow is written on each earnest face :
  '" *Memento Domine*," all them that mourn.'

In many a home, by rich or poor possessed,
The trembling mother prays (with tenderer care
Still clasping close her darling to her breast)—
  '" *Memento Domine*," old England's heir.'

Death brings us near akin ; the low, the great,
Alike must perish as the falling leaf;
Death levels all, he heeds nor wealth nor state—
  '" *Memento Domine*," all those in grief.'

No sceptred queen enthroned now fills each thought,
Death hath raised up deep living love to life ;
Rank, royalty, pass by as things of nought—
  '" *Memento Domine*," the sorrowing wife.'

'God save the Queen ! We put our trust in Thee,
And rev'rently in her great grief would share ;
Grant her Thy peace. " *Memento Domine*,"
  A nation's prayer.'

MY SOUL AND I.

LONG time ago, my Soul and I
Had many curious disquisitions
Upon the present and the past,
And on our relative positions.
And yet we failed, my Soul and I,
In proving our identity ;
For said I to my Soul, it seems
I should not be myself without you ;
Yet what you are, or whence you came,
Who can tell anything about you ?
Hadst waited long for me, my Soul,
Floating about in space infinite ?
Or did we two, created one,
Spring into life the self-same minute ?
How comes it that we suit so well—
Each so dissimilar in essence ;
One deathless, immaterial,
The other of corporeal presence ;

One born to die, one born to live,
The two yet needful for perfection ;
And birth the link, and death the sword,
That bind and loose the strange connection
Through which it haps my Soul and I
Are fashioned to Humanity ?

Dost thou not cling to me, my Soul,
With somewhat of a home-like feeling,
Whilst still I listen unto thee
For ever unknown worlds revealing ?
'Tis death to part from thee, my Soul ;
'Tis life to thee from me to sever ;
Must I decay ? must thou live on ?
And shall we parted be for ever ?
We've hoped and loved, and smiled and wept,
And tossed about the world together ;
May we not rest in Paradise
After our spell of rough earth weather ?
I cannot let thee go, my Soul,
We both must linger at the portal ;
The gates will not be opened wide
Until my dust be made immortal.
Then shall we be, my Soul and I,
Still one throughout eternity.

'JUSTUS FREIHERR VON LIEBIG IST GESTORBEN.'

ANOTHER master-spirit gone from earth!
Recalled by God, who through those dead lips spake
Strange revelation of His wondrous works;
For so doth God from time to time vouchsafe
To send the world fruit from that knowledge-tree,
Whose secrets Adam with fair Eden lost.
Recalled—ere yet relentless Time had pressed
With hand too heavy on his noble brow
Or dimmed the lustre of his intellect;
But whilst life's summer rays still ling'ring shone
In ripest glory round him, so he went
From earth; and left a mourning world behind.

   I looked upon the calm face of the dead,
All peaceful, sleeping 'midst the blooming flowers,
Whilst earthly honours glittered at his feet;
Given by kings to him, a greater king,
Crowned by the hand of God with God's own crown
Of kingship. Not o'er single realm to rule,

But o'er the greater empire of men's minds
Deathless to reign throughout all after-time
Wherever Science shall be known on earth.

And so I paid my homage to the dead,
Not for myself alone, but with the thought
Of my own sorrowing England and my Queen,
I laid my flowers upon the great man's bier.

Dead! and the world a-weeping! Dead! ah, nay,
Why weep ye for the dead? He hath but slept
Into a purer and more perfect life
Where the unknown is all made clear and plain,
And greater wonders day by day revealed
Than man in mortal nature can conceive;
For earthly film has fallen from his eyes
And not His works alone but God Himself
The soul immortal hath seen face to face.

Munich: 1873.

The room in which Baron von Liebig lay in state after his death
was a perfect mass of flowers. He was surrounded and almost covered
with the most beautiful wreaths, crosses, and bouquets of flowers,
flanked by a border of palms. He looked as if he were asleep, and his
eyebrows being very black and well-formed gave him a life-like ap-
pearance. There were white flowers on his breast and a small laurel
wreath on his head. On his breast also were some of his orders, and
other orders and decorations were lying in a brilliant heap at his feet.
Candles were burning around with bouquets in front of them.

THE FELLING OF THE TREES.

WITHIN the darkened room he lay
And heard the moaning wind go by;
And listening to the requiem sung, he knew that he
    must die.

The scent of pine woods faintly stole
Upon the languid summer breeze,
And sharp the woodman's axe told out the felling of
    the trees.

His thoughts from out the prisoned gloom
Went wandering into dreamy space,
Where through mossed stems gold shreds of light the
    fleeting shadows chase.

He saw the scarlet strawberries hide
'Neath unparched grass-waves green and cool,
He saw the shallow streamlet slip into the shady
    pool.

He knew each wood-path, memories sweet
Upfloated from a sun-gilt time ;
He knew each tree the woodman's axe felled in its
    leafy prime.

He listened all the long day through,
Another and another gone—
' So fall the mighty as the trees !   Ah Lord, Thy will
    be done ! '

He listened till the evening came,
And then the woodman's axe grew still,
And as the setting sun went down, he murmured
    ' 'Tis Thy will.'

And then the summer stars shone out,
And night across the heavens crept,
  And on his weary couch men thought the sleeper
    only slept ;—

But with red dawn they whispered low,
' Another to his rest is gone ! '
And still the woodman felled the trees, and still the
    busy world went on.

M

BRING ROSES.

BRING roses !
   Life is so fair ;
The world is golden-paven
   Everywhere.
Youth dips his white foot in the stream
   So slowly flowing ;
Life is a glorious dream
   Still growing
Into a fair reality.

Bring Roses !
   Life has grown dark ;
The river sullen rages,
   And no spark
Of sunlight flecks the waves, and wild
   The wind is blowing ;
The dream fled with the dawning ;
   Life is growing
Into a sad reality.

Bring Roses!
  For life is cold,
And lacks the beauty-woven
  Veil of old.
Scatter the swiftly ebbing tide
  With flowers a-glowing,
That mortals may not heed
  Its flowing
Unto a dark reality.

Bring Roses!
  For life hath fled;
Twine them with gold-eyed pansies
  For the dead,
Then stay thy hand, for Death hath brought
  Roses supernal;
Earth's dream is passed, and in
  Th' Eternal
Man finds a blest reality.

A REQUIEM.

(IN MEMORIAM.)

M. L. M G., OBIIT 1874.

FOR the belovèd one, whose death hath made
  A life-long death to linger in our breast ;
And in the silent grave, in sorrow laid
  Earth's hopes to rest.

For her, whose life was more than half our own,
  Forth-blossoming with rare and fragrant flowers,
That scarce we knew till Death the truth made known
  Or hers—or ours.

For her, whose life like some fair guiding star,
  Shed on our paths a never-failing light ;
Till o'er our heaven Death stretched a gloomy bar,
  And made all night :

We, waiting, listen for her voice in vain ;
  The work-day world enwrapped in silence seems ;
We long for night to clasp yet once again
  Her hand in dreams.

Our footsteps falter, and our song is hushed ;
  We pause, where the white summer roses wave :
Our hearts are buried there, our joys lie crushed
  Within that grave.

Alas ! the golden bowl is broken now,
  The silver cord is sudden snapped in twain,
And Death has set his signet on our brow,
  With cankering stain.

The world may robe itself in rainbow dyes,
  The birds may gaily sing, the buds unfold ;
Our ears are dull, a mist-veil shades our eyes—
  Our lives are cold.

Our souls unto the dust in anguish sore
  Are bowed, through severance of the tender tie,
And fast the bitter blinding tears down-pour
  In agony.

Ay weep! ay weep!   Our faith is none the less,
  Although in tears we give our hearts relief;
God's loving mercy we can yet confess
  Amidst our grief.

Ay weep! ay weep!   For God has given us tears,
  And hearts of flesh, that feel, that break, that bleed
He pities us—in heaven our cry He hears—
  He knows our need.

Kyrie Eleison.

O Christ, have mercy! Hearken to our cry!
Since Thou beside the grave where Lazarus slept,
Felt, in Thy Manhood, man's infirmity—
And, loving, wept.

O Lord! O Christ! have mercy! Thou didst heed,
And dried the tears the sorrowing widow shed:
Lord, Thou wilt not condemn us, if we plead
To mourn our dead.

O Lord! O Christ! have mercy! Thou dost know
Each throb and quiver of the wounded heart,
Each inly struggle to endure the blow ;
Thy strength impart.

Recordare.

O Lord, remember us ! Thy servants, when,
As to Thy Cross, we faint, and trembling cling ;
Pale death stands by, despite the power of men,
With folded wing.

Remember, Lord, Thy wandering footsore sheep,
Who, though oft-erring, strive to follow where
Thy voice is heard by healing waters deep,
In pastures fair.

O Lord, remember us ! Thou cam'st to save,
The power of man's last enemy to break,
Thou wilt not, in the passage of the grave,
Thine own forsake.

Thou didst remember, Lord, the dying thief;
And even so, when death shall close our eyes,
Remember, Lord! Bear us, beyond our grief,
To Paradise.

Hostias.

Praises and prayers in thankful sacrifice
Upon the altar of our hearts we lay ;
The grief-touched incense Thou wilt not despise,
Nor, turn away.

O Lord! we thank Thee, for our loved ones dead,
Whom Thou within Thy circling arms held fast,
As they, along the lonely vale o'erspread
With shadows, passed.

O Lord! we thank Thee for the pitying love,
That tenderly hewed out the path they trod,
Raising their souls, the joys of earth above,
Through peace with God.

O Lord! we thank Thee, in that Thou hast made
Their lives to us a precious chain of gold,
Whose links bind round us, whilst its clasp is laid
Within Thy hold.

We thank Thee, Lord, that underneath Thy feet,
Sin, Death, and Hell, Thou didst triumphant hurl,
And open flung, whilst angel-song rang sweet,
Heaven's gates of pearl.

We praise Thee, Lord, that though Death's flood divide,
We wait on Thee, one living army still;
Souls yearn alike on either side the tide
To do Thy Will.

O Lord! we give Thee thanks, that even now,
We, with the blessèd ones, to Thee may raise
Our song, and heaven and earth together bow
In fervent praise.

O Lord! O Lord! perchance it may be when
Earth's swelling anthem pierces through the skies,
Our loved may hear the mourners' far ' Amen!'
In Paradise.

N

Lux Aeterna.

From gorgeous flashing wall to turret high,
A city stands enthroned in wondrous light,
There blooming summer reigns eternally,
There—is no night.

And there no sun, no moon, no stars need shine,
For God's own glory fills the space around ;
The Lamb for ever is the Light Divine,
With honour crowned.

Fair through the city flows a crystal tide ;
Fadeless the flowers that on its banks are seen ;
Droop-down fruit-laden trees on either side,
In living green—

There in the morn that needs no light of sun,
Each wondering soul shall measure soul anew,
And deeds that earthly homage never won,
Meet guerdon true.

And many a one on earth, an unknown king,
There, crowned, shall find in God his dormant right ;
There shall the saved of nations honour bring,
And walk in light.

There shall be seen how sorrow's dimming blight,
And every weary step of suffering trod,
Led to the city of Eternal Light :
Led up to God.

O ! glorious Zion ! city, passing fair ;
O ! golden land ! O ! haven of the blest !
O God ! O God ! that we were with Thee there,
In perfect rest.

Cum Sanctis.

Lord ! grant, that when this troubled life is o'er,
To us the heritage be also given,
That with the holy ones, for evermore,
We dwell in heaven.

There by the glassy sea, with that great throng,
Who ' Holy ! Holy ! Holy ! ' ever cry ;
May we Thy praise in ceaseless strain prolong,
Throughout eternity.

　　　Amen !

LONDON : PRINTED BY
SPOTTISWOODE AND CO., NEW-STREET SQUARE
AND PARLIAMENT STREET

www.ingramcontent.com/pod-product-compliance
Lightning Source LLC
Chambersburg PA
CBHW020227030726
47497CB00009B/2986